DARK HORSES

The Magazine of Weird Fiction

MAY | 2023

No. 16

Copyright © 2023 Hobb's End Press. All Rights Reserved. Published by Hobb's End Press, a division of ACME Sprockets & Visions. Cover design Copyright © 2023 Wayne Kyle Spitzer. All stories Copyright © 2023 by their respective authors. Please direct all inquiries to: HobbsEndBooks@yahoo.com

CONTENTS

A BROTHERHOOD OF IDIOTS
Arthur Davis

THE ABYSS OF FEAR
Nick Young

AN EVEN GREATER WOMAN
Victoria Male

EASY PREY
Terry Sanville

THAT THING WE KILLED
Wayne Kyle Spitzer

GATE K22
John Stadelman

JUST A LITTLE TASTE
Samantha Lee Curran

JUST ADD WATER
Bill Link

NEW YOU NANCY DREW
Chloé Sehr

DAN THE TRUMPET MAN
Mary Jo Rabe

A BROTHERHOOD OF IDIOTS

Arthur Davis

Gracie and Larkin are splayed out behind the dumpster and have been holding hands since I got here. Neither has moved in a month.

The flow of broken humanity into and out of this old, bombed-out toy factory never stops. Those that find this place share an instant identity.

We are all idiots.

It was the gas. It was always the gas.

Small as it is, the best part of this factory is what remains of the large corrugated roof. It's been battered and crumpled. Ravaged from generations of war, petty conflicts and weather. Whenever it rains, as it does for a few minutes every day, a legion of wandering trickles collects into a steady single stream. We run with broken pans and bottles and collect water any way we can.

I don't recall what I did yesterday or the day or week before. I know that I've been to other encampments. I have a deep bruise on my right shoulder. Cuts from long ago can be traced along both legs, and my right side hurts when I breathe deeply. So I know I can't run. Hopefully, whoever might want to track me down in the future will not notice.

I examine my clothing in the hope of finding a scrap of paper or a tag that will tell me anything about me, other than what I've seen in broken mirrors these long, many years. Where was I from? Where was the last battle of the last conflict and what remains of humanity?

"Jesus, you do that every day and you ain't found nothing yet," Carruthers said in a haze of depression. He broke a bone in his foot kicking an empty fifty-five-gallon drum last week. He called the drum, "Doreen." He's tall and lanky and has a fierce hate for everyone. I've seen that look before. Everyone has.

He calls out "Doreen" a few times a day and as often in his sleep, as if to remind himself what he once had, or once failed to grasp, and apparently doesn't regret that his outburst has left him nearly crippled, so great and unresolved is his anger. He hops around to grab his share of water and screams about his pain and Doreen. A few look up when he passes. Most are asleep or half dead or long dead.

Only the rats know the exact count.

There are about thirty of us. Maybe a few more. Huddled together in what remains of the bombed out toy factory. Many arrive with old wounds. Scars. I stopped counting mine some time ago. I inhale until the pain is too much. The gas can do that. It scrambles your brain and makes you believe that the horrors of your past are nothing compared to those of your future.

Hard as I try, I can't recall ever having played with a toy. There are scraps of colored plastic toy pieces and long-faded brochures scattered about. They're nice to look at and read whenever I recognize a few words. I don't recall ever having played with a toy.

Maybe that's what makes me an idiot, or maybe inhaling the gas is to blame? If I could remember what toys looked like and my connection to them, maybe I would be more than an idiot? I don't know what someone is called if they're more than an idiot. But I'd like to think it matters.

Sometimes I fantasize what it would be like being more than an idiot. I used to fantasize a lot more years ago. I even tried to scrape off and sand off and burn off the little red star on the top of both hands. They were put there for a purpose. Everyone here has the same little red stars and knows what they mean. And never forgets why and how they got there.

We are a brotherhood of idiots.

"Long?" I said, as surprised as Carruthers.

"What about long?"

"What about long?" I said for no apparent reason. "I think it's better than short."

"Yeah. You're right."

"Everything long is longer than most things that are short?"

Carruthers winced himself through the pain and sat up straight. "I never thought of it that way."

"Anyone got something to eat?" Carol said. She paused and walked on to the next clot of survivors. That's what she does all day. Then it strikes me that she has the energy to stand and walk must mean she has found food somewhere around here. Maybe there is enough for two. But I can't be that obvious. People pick up on the slightest differences from one day to another.

"Long? Longing? Longin?" I repeated.

Carruthers doesn't hear. He fell back asleep. His ankle already swelled into a harsh blue softball. I don't think he realizes what the next few days will bring. Maybe that's a good thing. Even Doreen wouldn't be able to help him.

Who the hell is Longin and why does the name keep coming back to me? Was he a friend? A relative? Someone who was going to meet me somewhere? Maybe I didn't make it there on time, so he left and took all my hope with him?

"My brother had long toes." I said, surprised as Carruthers.

"You remember that? How can you?"

"It just came to me." It was the gas talking. It twists facts and compromises memory. Who knew what the truth was anymore. And, even if you did, what difference would it make when you had no future.

"But it can't. It shouldn't. I can't remember a thing like that. No one here can remember anything like that," he said getting agitated.

Carruthers kept a steady eye on me. It made me uncomfortable. I didn't need him spreading around suspicions.

"I once killed a man with my own hands," Carruthers said that evening, examining them in front of his face. "Killed him like he was nothing. Like everyone is nothing, and I had had enough of him and his jokes and bragging and he wouldn't stop talking so he needed killing and everyone applauded when he slipped out of my hands and fell to the floor of the shit-covered bar. It was long ago and, hey, maybe that's our connection? Long? Long ago? Were you in the bar the night I killed him? The cops were looking for witnesses, but my friends never turned on me."

The last time it rained, he told this same story. But there was something more to it then. More violence. More details about how he had brutally murdered a young stranger were missing in this version.

Now I am remembering when I shouldn't be.

"That's where the woman was being harassed by two men? They wouldn't stop bothering her? You got between them and her and they started a fight. You hit one so hard he fell, and the other came at you and you grabbed him by the throat as he kept hitting you. You told me that story before. Most men would have left the woman to her tormentors. Not you. You were the brave one."

Carruthers hesitated. "I thought you were there. One of the witnesses who the cops missed."

"I only know what you told me before. I believed every word of it."

Carruthers fell back against the wall, satisfied that the ending to this tale was like the last few times he had told it to me for the first time. As long as he was the hero, he would be satisfied until the next time he needed to remind himself, and anyone else, that he still mattered.

That his existence still had meaning.

The toes on my right foot are completely exposed through my shoe. They're filthy. Everyone's feet are filthy. We all wear shoes from the dead that never fit, no matter how many we try on. It's hot out. Maybe July or August. Two of the twelve months I like best. Since I remembered there were twelve months in a year could I be more than an idiot?

I've heard people being called morons and imbeciles. I'm sure I once knew what they meant. Are morons or imbeciles better or worse than idiots?

I don't like the word *moron*.

If I am more than an idiot, I can't let on. No one will talk to me. Some will turn on me, or worse. They will figure that I am a threat to our small group. If I were them and I found out, I would kill me in my sleep. I have to be careful. I can't let anyone know about Longin either. If I figure out who he is and what he meant to me, they will smell it. Sense it. Fear it.

"Longin," I whispered a few times until the only thing I felt were my dry, cracked lips.

Two women are huddled at the far end of the factory floor. It's cooler down there. It's open to the wind and the rail yards behind them. From anywhere all round, someone could see most of them both. Then why would they take a slice of risk, and what do they know about where they are sitting, or are they hiding right in front of us?

Maybe being an idiot has advantages. The smarter you are the more you know, and the more you know, you realize you can't know everything.

Like, what has become of civilization? "What's become of civilization?"

Where did that word come from? I liked the way it sounded.

And I don't trust Carruthers anymore. There is something unsettling about him. He wants something. Everybody here wants something but him most of all.

Except for a few scraps of food, I don't want anything. I have been here a long time and can't remember where I was before. I don't seem to be as needy or wounded. I don't think I'm as desperate as most in this small encampment.

It's starting to drizzle. You can hear the tentative patter of raindrops on the twisted corrugated roofing. A few of the strongest start to crawl, cups and bottles in hand, toward the artificial spout from which God has provided us with enough water to subsist.

He should know all about us and how much time each of us has left on earth. But what if he's walking among us? What if God is here watching each of us? God would surely have to be an idiot to let mankind sink to such a sorry state and desperate despair.

"What about civilization?" Carruthers whispered from deep in his sleep.

Maybe God is an idiot too? That makes him no better than any of us. Maybe he is less than an idiot? That would make him an inferior, as Carruthers says of the rest of the squalor into which we have all congealed.

"Unless, of course, I am God," I said with a resonance in my voice I never heard.

And it woke Carruthers.

"God? You're really God," he said loudly and, gasping for air, scrambled to his knees. "I knew it all long," he shouted to the others. Their heads turned. Their eyes popped with excitement and suspicion.

Carruthers held on to a nearby beam and pulled himself erect. I couldn't recall when I had seen him this tall. His passion had overcome the excruciating pain in his ankle, or was that my doing so he could celebrate my unveiling? I wanted to say something, then decided to let the moment pass as I knew it would when the half-asleep madman fell back to the ground.

I was wrong.

"You're really God?" one old man asked, offering up his half-filled bottle of filthy water. "You're the one who did this," Carruthers said dragging his ruined foot toward me.

"He's been God all the time while he watched us suffer and die."

"I never believed in a god," a woman so tattered and filthy her face was recognizable, said.

I struggled to stand and explain the misunderstanding but never got that far before the first bottle struck the side of my head. The second missed, but a rock found my right cheek and sent me falling into a pile of rags.

I took a panicked breath and gagged. The rags must have once been soaked in a toxic chemical mix. By my second breath, my lungs started to burn. The hail of outrage above grew louder. I was being battered by sticks and clubs and bottles and rocks from head to feet. The voices grew in number and outrage and resentment as my head slipped deeper into the toxic pile.

"No," I managed a mutter, though mostly to myself.

"Look at what he has done to us, to the whole world," a woman railed.

"He is responsible for this," another, younger, voice rang out right above me.

"God's here, among us, to save us from further suffering," an old man shouted in protest.

"He's God," came from many failing souls.

"I know him. We once talked, and he never told me he was God," someone said.

The rage of voices and bottles, rocks, and sticks were all over me. They struck and struck and crashed down against muscle, bone, and fiber. The right side of my face was covered in blood from a crack in my skull.

Now, whoever I am no longer matters.

I caught a quick glimpse of the two women who were sitting at the end of the factory. They were watching from a distance. They were twins. I thought that wonderful. Maybe one or both knew Longin?

Someone kicked my ribs. Another followed, but by this time the pain had lessened. I became thankful but had no way to express my gratitude to the mob for taking the last breath from my lungs, the last drop of blood from my heart, the last vestige of hope I had been accumulating for so long.

And then, slowly, the voices faded, the wave of abuse became a distant, unthreatening sensation. I was being saved by the absolute certainty of a coming darkness.

Beautiful, welcoming, life-giving darkness.

So, this is how I die, or is it merely a first step toward being resurrected?

That meant I would be back.

Just, hopefully, not here where faith was long lost.

"Long. Lost?" I said before what remained of the world collapsed on me.

The missing piece of the puzzle revealed itself as a final blow struck the back of my head. I was on my way home. Shortly to return healed. Holy. Eternally forgiving and never again wanting.

The gas had peeled back the mystery of my past and exposed me as the only true God.

THE ABYSS OF FEAR

Nick Young

In the late evening sky to the west, a canopy of ugly indigo thunderheads crowded the tree line. Beneath the ragged edge of clouds the sky shone with a sickly glow. August was just beginning to nudge its way into autumn, and a sudden stillness had fallen, signaling that a hell of a storm was brewing up to disrupt Wellesley's leafy peace.

On Pond Road, in an especially cloistered corner of the town, headlights speared the lowering gloom as a Range Rover topped a rise, banked around a gentle leftward curve and braked at a driveway entrance leading to a large Georgian colonial set back seventy-five yards from the street. As the SUV pulled in, a gust of wind shuddered through the old maples lining the broad driveway. Lightning strobed the scene, catching the first of three garage bays on the east side of the house as it glided open.

Once inside, the Range Rover's engine was cut and the driver's door opened. Out stepped Rachel Oppenheim, still trim in her late forties, with close-cropped salt-and-pepper hair. Her clothes were expensive earth tones, suburban-casual, and she moved in them with easy grace, the legacy of her youth at the barre. A low rumble of thunder welled up from the distance, and she counted herself lucky to have made it home from the market before the full force of the storm hit. On any other Friday night, she wouldn't have been out at all; but there had been too many distractions that had piled up in the middle of the week, so she had been forced to put off her regular Whole Foods pilgrimage.

And she was still distracted, chiding herself for not touching base sooner with Phyllis Schwartz about September's discussion topics for the reading group at temple. While that was occupying her mind, she had reached the back of the SUV before the incessant chiming from inside reminded her that she'd left her door open and the key in the ignition. With an exasperated shake of her head, Rachel popped the Range Rover's rear hatch and began wrestling with two canvas totes filled with groceries.

She did not notice in the harsh light cast from overhead the shadow that had fallen behind her.

"Need a hand?"

The voice, a flat baritone, nearly caused Rachel to jump out of her skin. As she spun around, screaming once, the bags fell from her hands, sending their contents scattering across the concrete floor.

The man who stepped into the garage accompanied by a fresh burst of lightning was unremarkable in most respects. Thirty-ish, of medium height and build, he was dressed head-to-toe in black. In one hand he carried a leather bag to match. His face, with its Mediterranean complexion, was a mask of cold appraisal.

Nonchalantly, followed by the woman's terrified eyes, he set his bag down, turned and pushed a button on a wall control panel triggering the bay door to close slowly. Panic gripped Rachel, and now the ignition chime was no longer a simple annoyance but a hammering counterpoint to the pounding of her heart that she felt was ready to explode. Her breath came in short, choked gasps.

The intruder savored her fear, and the pleasure it gave him showed on his face as a wisp of a smile played at the corners of his mouth. He sauntered to the open door of the SUV, reached inside and pulled out the key. The sudden silence was jarring, even more chilling to Rachel. It screamed inside her head. She opened her mouth to speak, but fear trapped the words at the back of her throat. She forced herself to try again.

"Who are you?" The intruder didn't answer. Instead, with a casualness that only added to Rachel's growing dread, he meandered in front of her, surveying the interior of the spacious garage.

"In due time, Mrs. O. All in due time," he said, stopping and turning toward her. "You know, you're not being a very gracious hostess."

Rachel's brain raced, trying to control her panic, to make sense of the suffocating trap she was in and to find some way, any way, out of it.

"What do you mean?" she said, her voice ragged. A look of feigned hurt passed over the intruder's face.

"You're not going to invite me in?" A fresh spasm of terror tightened its grip on Rachel's throat.

"Please . . . " the word barely escaped her lips. He regarded her for a long moment, the manufactured charm quickly evaporating from his face.

"Let's go," he said, the ice returning to his voice. "Inside."

There was only a short distance to the door leading into the house, just a few steps, but Rachel had to summon whatever strength she still felt to will her rubbery legs to move. She turned the doorknob and stepped inside the mud room.

Tentatively she reached toward the home security system keypad on the wall, fighting to stop her fingers from shaking. But as she was about to tap in the first number of the code, her captor shot out a black-gloved hand and tightly encircled her wrist.

Rachel froze.

"I need to disable the system," she said hoarsely, "before it triggers the alarm."

"Make sure you don't enter an intruder code, Mrs. O. We wouldn't want a visit from the cops. I'd better see this little 'disarm' light turn green. Am I clear?" She nodded numbly, finishing the short sequence of numbers as a deafening crack of thunder rattled the house to its foundation. Rachel jumped, her knees buckling. The intruder rolled his eyes heavenward and then toward his captive. "It looks like we're really in for it," he said, with the barest hint of a smile. "Time to go, Mrs. O.

He put his hand at the small of Rachel's back, nudging her forward and through the open door to the kitchen. The room sprawled in front of them, dominated in its center by a large granite-topped island overhung by a heavy cast-iron rack festooned with copper cookware. The ebbing twilight shrouded the room in deepening shadows, with the only illumination the faint glow from accent lights under a bank of oak cabinets. Despite the coolness of the room, to Rachel the air hung oppressively, crackling with menace and the power of the building storm, and she fought to draw breath.

"Sit down over there," the intruder ordered, motioning toward the island. Unsteadily, Rachel crossed the room and slowly slid onto a tall chair while her captor walked to the opposite side and set his bag on the countertop. "You like storms, Mrs. O.?" She didn't reply, fearful that he was subjecting her to some kind of twisted test and that giving the wrong answer would only make the situation that much worse for her. Instead, she watched as the intruder closed his eyes and slowly tilted his head back. She could not know by the placid look on his face that jagged images of violent assault on another

17

storm-wracked night flashed through his mind with blinding speed. As if entering a bottomless black pool, he allowed himself to slide into its darkness. And the deeper he slipped, the greater his agony as the shards of memory cut into him.

After a long moment, Rachel summoned up enough courage to speak weakly:

"If you want money . . . " At first, there was no response; but slowly the intruder's eyes fluttered open, and he returned to the moment.

"What? he muttered.

"I said if you want money . . . jewelry — whatever you want. I'll give you anything."

But instead of responding immediately, he turned his attention to his bag, unzipping it and removing small, round candles, arraying them on the countertop before Rachel.

"Do you take me for a common thief?" he replied, his voice feigning aggrievement. "I am offended, Mrs. O." Now her raw fear and anxiety boiled over.

"*Stop calling me that!*" she snapped. "My name is Rachel — Rachel Oppenheim . . . and this is *my house!*" But her outburst had no effect. He continued to stare with nothing but coldness and calculation in his faint smile. Rachel's body sagged, her fury spent, and she said softly, "Just tell me what you want."

For a long moment he said nothing. Then, with the deliberation of a snake about to strike, the intruder inched his face across the island until it was close enough for her to recoil, twisting away from the moist sourness of his breath.

"Matches," he said evenly. "I want matches." Through the haze of her dread, Rachel wasn't certain she'd heard correctly.

"Matches?"

"That's right, matches . . . Mrs. O."

"The bottom drawer, right-hand side."

He bent, slid the drawer open and began searching.

At that moment, Rachel's terror sent her spinning back in time more than forty years to an episode that had branded a fear that had lurked deep within her psyche all the days of her life.

It was late Halloween afternoon, 1956. She had just turned five and was being watched by her eight-year-old brother Benny while their mother went to the grocery store to pick up more candy for the expected hordes of trick-or-treaters. She wouldn't be gone long, she had told her children, sternly admonishing Benny not to get into any mischief.

Many times in the past Benny had been given the same warning, and many times he had ignored it. So, no sooner had his mother left than he started in.

As the little girl stared wide-eyed, he told her that the two of them needed to try on their costumes before Mommy took them out that evening and that in order to do it the right way, they had to go down to the basement, to a "secret room." At first she resisted, telling her brother that it was too early to get dressed up, that Mommy would help them after supper, right before they went out around the neighborhood. But Benny persisted and was very persuasive, so Rachel took the small plastic package containing her costume when Benny thrust it toward her, and she allowed him to take her by the hand and lead her down the twelve steps to the basement.

It was a place she didn't like, a place she said was "cweepy" — damp and cloying — with its one dim lightbulb smelling of must and chemicals. Benny knew the basement scared his sister — that was part of what he was up to — so he held her hand tightly and kept telling her everything was alright, that he was protecting her. She was trusting, lulled by his reassuring words as he led her across the rough concrete floor to a doorway next to the worn workbench where their father kept his tools and sometimes tinkered with old clocks.

"Okay, Punky, this is it," Benny told her. "We'll go into Dad's closet, our most secret, secret hiding place — for you and me — nobody else. That's where we put on our Halloween stuff, okay? You go first while I wait out here."

She didn't want to go by herself. The closet wasn't that big, and there was only a tiny light. And it smelled bad from the oily rags and turpentine. Rachel didn't like it at all, but Benny kept pushing her, telling her not to be afraid, to "act like a big girl."

So she trusted him. She went in, clutching the plastic pouch with the little witch costume her mother had bought for her at the Ben Franklin. He shut the door behind her.

And then he turned out the light.

Being plunged into blackness sent a wave of fright through Rachel right away, but she tried her hardest not to scream, to act like a big girl. Instead, she called her brother's name — once, twice and again, louder each time. But Benny didn't answer her. He was standing outside the door, holding both hands over his mouth to stifle the laughter from what he thought was his best prank yet.

Inside the closet, Rachel's fear was beginning to overcome her. She was starting to gasp for breath. Tears were welling up in her eyes.

And then she heard the scratching near her feet and felt something clutch at the sock on her right foot and begin climbing up her ankle.

She panicked and began shrieking at the top of her lungs, kicking out her feet and hammering her bunched, tiny fists against the inside of the door for all she was worth.

Still, it didn't open right away. The agonizingly long moments dragged on, with more screaming, more helpless pounding as Benny stood, bent double with glee.

At that instant, salvation arrived with a clatter of shoes on the wooden stairs. Mother had returned from the store, heard the horrible screams and rushed down to the basement.

"My God, Benjamin, what have you done?" she shouted, tearing open the closet door and gathering Rachel into her arms, soothing her, cooing to her that she was safe, that "everything's alright now."

But everything wasn't alright for Rachel. She overcame the immediate trauma. Her brother was forced to make a sheepish, half-hearted apology, and the incident gradually receded with time.

But for Rachel, in the deepest part of her, that closet, that dark hole with its sickening smells and the skittering thing climbing her leg lurked like a latent virus. It had surfaced sporadically over the years in nightmares. But she always managed to rebury the terror, never fully acknowledging it, not even during her short time in therapy years before.

Now, it was back.

It was not a dream, and Rachel realized she could not push away the horror as she always had. Mother would not rescue her this time.

She must find a way to do it for herself.

And so, as she pulled herself back to the moment, Rachel's eyes darted to the countertop where, an arm's length from her, a hardwood block bristled with knives. In that instant, she saw a chance — perhaps the only one — to fight back. She gathered herself, breathing raggedly, and screwed up enough courage to begin stealing her left hand across the cool granite. But just as she snatched one of the large knives from the block, nerves got the better of her, and the knife slipped from her fingers, clattering to the floor. The intruder straightened up, matches in hand. He laid the matchbox on the island and retrieved the knife, slowing sliding it back into its slot.

"You know, you really should try to be more careful with fine cutlery." Rachel, angry at her failure of nerve, her fear surging, lashed out.

"Oh, God — *enough with the banalities already!*" The intruder looked at his captive for a long moment before nodding.

"You're right, Mrs. O. Time to get down to business."

Swiftly, he took up the matches and lit the candles, then reached into his bag and removed a coil of rope. A fresh wave of terror washed over Rachel.

"Look," she pleaded, "whatever it is you want, take it — and you can be gone long before my husband gets home."

21

The intruder had moved behind Rachel and, with a sure hand, began binding her to the chair. As he did so, she let out an anguished sob.

"Why Mrs. O., surely you haven't forgotten that your husband's not coming home tonight," he said as he went about his task. "This is his big weekend at Yale. Now, I'm not much of a gambler, but I'm betting that you wish you'd gone with him, even though you loathe the way he gets when he's the center of attention. And he most certainly will be, especially once he presents his paper tomorrow." He affected a grand tone: "The Precursors of Criminal Behavior — Paradigms in the Diagnosis of Sociopathology." Then his voice dripped with bile: "Doctor Sidney Oppenheim, the fucking toast of academe." Rachel's eyes widened at this display of venom.

"Does Sidney know you?"

"I think not," her captor replied, removing his leather gloves and replacing them with a latex pair he drew from his bag. "But he should. And he will." A long burst of lightning was followed quickly by rattling thunder. The first big drops of wind-driven rain staccatoed across the kitchen windows.

The intruder dipped into his bag once more and withdrew an oblong case of dark, polished wood trimmed in brass. "Are you a collector?" he asked casually, carefully setting the case on the countertop. Rachel could not take her eyes from the object, not wanting to contemplate what might be inside.

"What?" Again, barely a whisper.

"A collector — stamps, coins . . . ?"

"No."

"That's a pity," he replied, unsnapping the latch on the case and lifting the lid. "Now I have a passion for these." He turned the case toward Rachel, who strained against the rope holding her and shuddered at the contents — a wicked array of vintage surgical instruments, cold and deadly in the sharp flashes of lightning and flickering candlelight. Slowly, he removed a foot-long saw from the red-velvet lining and displayed it lovingly. "Ebony handles . . . chromed steel — a Civil War field amputation kit, Mrs. O. Superb workmanship. Incredibly sharp. Absolutely vital in the days before anesthesia." He replaced the saw and withdrew a long Liston knife. "Did you know that a skilled surgeon using these could remove a man's entire leg in less than thirty seconds?" As he finished, he turned a malevolent eye toward Rachel as his words sunk in.

"Please — *oh, God!*" she pleaded as, knife still in hand, he began slowly circling the island. "What did my husband do to you? What do you want with me? *Please* — I'll do anything . . . " She was struggling with all the strength she had left, desperately trying to keep him in her field of vision " . . . just don't hurt me!"

He stopped directly behind her. Eyes closed, he lifted his head toward the roiling heavens. Once more, his mind was assailed by a barrage of violent images.

"*Please . . . !*"

He opened his eyes — flat, utterly without feeling. The tableau froze in a jagged streak of lightning.

AN EVEN GREATER WOMAN

Victoria Male

Now:
"So how did you two meet?" the interviewer, NBC's Nisha Jones, asked. She feigned familiarity by lowering her voice a fraction, as if she was asking just the two of them. As if she, Vivika, and Adam weren't all mic'd and surrounded by a film crew and senior publicists.

Vivika and Adam reflexively looked at one another, the classic "who's going to tell it this time?" deliberation between couples.

Adam squeezed her hand. The action shifted her knuckles ever so slightly so that several carats of diamonds Vivika wore on her left finger glinted under the studio lights. "Viv? Wanna take this one?"

She nodded with the grin she'd plastered on her face since they took their seats on the studio's canvas chairs. "Sure. It was our last year at Stanford, and it just so happened that we were both camped out in the same corner of the library when Adam broke his laptop–"

"Excuse me, the laptop broke, I had nothing to do with it."

"And still you threw a very public temper tantrum at three in the morning–" Nisha chuckled at Viv's quip.

"My dissertation was due in three hours."

"So I offered to help him with his plight - his hissy fit was incredibly distracting." "Plus I promised to buy her breakfast after I submitted the paper–"

"And we've been inseparable ever since," Vivica finished, her eyes fond and trained on Adam, their story so well-practiced it had begun to feel true.

Nisha matched Viv's grin. "During that breakfast, did either of you have even the slightest inkling that you'd go on to found the most prolific tech company of the past decade?"

"If I had those types of inklings I would've foregone school altogether and made some strategic investments in the stock market," Adam chuckled, his self-effacing charm irresistible to Nisha, the camera's unrelenting lens, and even after seven years together, to Vivika. "But we knew that together we'd make something special."

"Special is an understatement. Brahman's self-driving Ratha cars have ranked as the safest in their class for the past three years and running. Since the introduction of the Ikshana robot, the success rate of open-heart surgeries has improved by twenty-six percent in the hospitals with access to the technology, and three in four households worldwide employ the Dasa AI assistant in their households. Popular Mechanics named you the 'First Couple of the Future.' That's quite the title."

"Certainly Nisha, and at the risk of sounding arrogant, it fits," Adam did sound arrogant, but he was so dynamic that it didn't matter. "While we're incredibly proud of everything we and the team at Brahman have accomplished, we're just getting started."

"Vivika – not only are you the COO of Brahman, you're married to the CEO, and you're both parents to a four-year-old daughter, Minerva. How on Earth do you balance it all?"

Viv was a consummate professional. She was too smart, too used to this, to allow the sting of the question to register on her features. She knew exactly how to guide her response back to business, but before Viv could utter a word, Adam interjected, "Viv is the brains of Brahman, the most sophisticated artificial intelligence on Earth. Surely you're not only going to ask her questions about her marriage?"

She returned Adam's squeeze of the hand in silent gratitude.

Nisha masked her humiliation with a shit-eating grin. "You're right. My apologies, Vivika."

"Thank you, and please, call me Viv."

"Given that you're the brains and beauty behind the company's cutting-edge technology, can you give us any clues as to what Brahman has in store at your annual Praksepana launch event later this week?"

Viv's smile turned a modicum more genuine, they were back on track. "You'll have to tune in and see, but I will say that what we announce on Friday has the potential to make a major positive impact on society, and continue our mission to disrupt the status quo in order to make the world a better place to live in for all."

"And Adam, you're giving the keynote address at the event, which is regularly one of the most highly anticipated and scrutinized talks in tech all year. How do you cope with the pressure and the fact that there will be billions of people watching you?"

"It's all energy, we're all energy," Adam began, "So what I strive for is…" "Is what?"

But Adam didn't answer. He sat there paralyzed, his mouth frozen around the next word he'd intended to speak. Viv's stomach swooped, she knew they shouldn't have done this live, but Raj had promised her, and it hadn't happened in ages–

"Honey?" Viv prompted him, trying to keep her voice from betraying the ice-cold fear sluicing through her veins. "Adam?"

Still nothing. The lights became blinding and the sound of Viv's blood thundering in her ears battled with the phantom mechanical whir that seemed to be getting louder with each passing millisecond.

Nisha looked to Viv, "Is he alright?"

"Yes, yes, he's fine," she was trying to convince herself just as much as Nisha. "He hasn't been sleeping...between the event and Minnie, he's running on fumes–"

Off-camera, it was chaos. Lindsay gesticulated wildly in an attempt to get Viv's attention, which was not helping, and the set medic was called. Viv continued to vamp while she slipped two fingers under where Adam's arm rested to touch the inside of his wrist. She tapped the date of their anniversary - October 2nd, 10 rapid taps, then 2 slow ones - on his pulse, silently cursing Raj to hell and back.

The set medic got closer. Nisha decided it was time to intervene. "Vivika, I think we should–"

"–to use it, channel it, you see. Doesn't matter if I'm reading my daughter a bedtime story about doing Brahman's annual keynote."

"Are you alright?" A flabbergasted Nisha inquired. Viv knew what she was thinking: what the fuck had just happened?

Adam flashed her a dazzling, completely oblivious, grin. "Yes, why wouldn't I be?

"You spaced out for a sec there, honey," Viv leaned into the trope of the exasperated wife. "You became a total glazed doughnut on national television, so now will you listen to me and take it a little easier?"

Vivika manufactured a laugh so loud and domineering that Adam and Nisha had no choice but to join in.

"You have a mimosa waiting for me, right?" were Viv's first words to Lindsay after they cut to commercial and stepped off set.

"You and me both," Lindsay was never one to miss a beat, "and the world's strongest espresso for Adam since he cannot pull that shit at Good Morning America in thirty."

Viv ground her teeth and glanced back at where her husband was expertly waving off any medical attention. "How bad is it?"

"It's fine," Lindsay effaced. Viv shot her publicist an unconvinced frown. "Seriously. It's already being memed - 'me when I don't have my coffee' and stuff like that. We'll make it work for us, if anything it shows Adam is only human, right?"

Viv shrugged noncommittally and presented her palm for Lindsay to place her phone back in.

She wasn't surprised to see the explosion of texts from Raj. She neglected to read any of them and simply sent: You swore to me it wouldn't happen again.

Raj's reply was instant. I know. When do you finish press?

Adam caught up with her before Viv could answer Raj. "I'm sorry."

Viv didn't look up from her phone as they trailed Lindsay back to the green room, "I told you to get some rest."

"I know, and I said I'm sorry," he countered, then stopped her in the hallway. "Come on, please?"

He didn't deserve her anger. The fuckup back there wasn't Adam's fault. "Just promise me your keynote is going to be incredible. And you'll come to bed before 2 tonight."

"You know the keynote is always incredible. And better yet, I'll wake you up to see the sun rise."

"3 AM, best and final."

"You drive a hard bargain Mrs. Vateri." "That's boss-woman to you."

Lindsay watched Viv surrender to a rare public display of affection with her husband, a smirk playing on her lips. Vivika

Vateri was a certified genius, a born hustler, and a shark in the boardroom, but she was silly-putty when it came to Adam.

When their lips separated, Viv murmured a barely audible "thank you" to her husband.

Adam regarded her with a puzzled expression. "For sticking up for me back there."

"'Course. You're my wife, and besides, it's the truth."

Then:

"Fuck!!!" Vivika slammed her fist with such force onto the rickety bistro table it sent both her and Raj's coffees flying, not to mention drew the attention of those surrounding in the cafe. "Sorry. I'll buy you another one-"

"No, let me get it," he insisted, already rising.

Viv called out a weak thanks while she stared at yet another rejection email from yet another VC sitting in her inbox When Raj returned with two fresh beverages, he was ready to commiserate. "What's wrong with these guys?"

It was, quite literally, the billion dollar question. Viv's advisors at Stanford had never seen an AGI - Artificial General Intelligence - so intelligent. They believed that Viv would be the first to crack Artificial Super Intelligence. They happily opened their proverbial black books for her, reaching out to their friends in high places, all ready to ride the hell out of Viv's coattails and take credit for "discovering" her.

At least that's what was supposed to happen. What actually happened was twenty seven rejections. Apparently no one wanted to invest in who the Stanford computer science department had anointed as the frontrunner for producing machine consciousness.

Fissures spread through Raj's heart at the sight of his best friend trying not to cry. Viv was tough as nails, but what she was going through was brutal.

"Okay well, fuck them, we'll get super drunk tonight-"

"But you have work tomorrow-"

"We'll get super drunk tonight and then what's your next move? Who are you waiting to hear back from?"

Viv wilted at the question. "This was the last one - Sapphire."

The din from the coffee shop overtook their conversation for a few moments before Viv shook herself out of it. "Think you can put in a good word for me at AAB?"

"Before you throw in the towel on revolutionizing society, maybe try a couple of cold emails."

"Why Raj? So I can clog my inbox with more 'respectful passes'?" Viv took a sip of her fresh latte and a single, humorless laugh escaped her. "I know I'm preaching to the choir here, but 'inclusivity in tech'? More specifically, 'women in tech'? What a load of bullshit. I hate Elizabeth Holmes. You know, if I were a man-"

Viv stopped mid-sentence and her eyes brightened the longer she gazed at Raj. He was not proud of how the length of her stare had a direct correlation to his heart rate. "What?"

"I'm not a man, but you are." "Yeah, last I checked."

"And you're brilliant. I'll cold email all of Silicon Valley if you come on as co-founder.

You won't have to lift a finger, I promise, I literally just need your dick."

Viv's words would've been music to Raj's ears if they'd been spoken, or better moaned, in a different context. "Viv, I can't."

"Why not?" she demanded. "You just said I'm going to revolutionize society! I'm your best friend! One of those two reasons usually would suffice for most!"

"My contract," he murmured.

"Oh come on Raj, stop being such a boy scout. You're going to break it as soon as the Dasa robot is ready for seed capital."

"Exactly. Minerva AI is your dream and Dasa is mine. Plus, you don't need me."

"Actually, I do!" Viv regrouped, desperately trying to prevent her frustration from getting the best of her. "Take me out of this. You're really going to let Russia and China beat us? You're going to let our enemies control the future because of a stupid contract that engineers break all the time?!"

Viv had a point. But still, Raj hesitated.

"Okay maybe you need me, but you don't want me," Raj amended himself. "I don't want to be shoehorned in-"

"You wouldn't be! My God, if I got funding, Dasa would be our first launch!"

Raj wanted Viv to want him for more than launching her tech empire. It occurred to him that this could be the moment that he finally told her how he felt. Raj gathered his courage and-

"No one takes me seriously." Defiant tears returned to Viv's eyes. She stood and determinedly packed away her phone, sunglasses, and laptop.

"Don't go," Raj pleaded softly. He told himself she hadn't heard him as Viv stormed out of the cafe.

Now:

Viv was surprised to find Adam in their bedroom after she'd kissed Minnie goodnight. She'd figured that she wouldn't see him until 2:59 AM at the earliest, and fully expected to spend the next few hours with her laptop and a glass or three of wine.

However, Adam was undressing when she padded inside. Viv took a moment to study him, to luxuriate in each new swath of caramel skin he revealed as he shed his clothes. "Fancy seeing you here."

Adam stalked toward her the way a lion does when it spots a tasty-looking gazelle. "Hi." "You took my advice."

"I always take your advice."

"No you don't, but that's alright. It's one of the things I love about you."

Adam pulled her to him, inhaling deeply to catch the lingering scent of the perfume she dabbed at the crack of dawn before they left to do the morning shows. He kissed her neck, then stripped off her blouse.

"Oh, this is why you're not holed up in your office."

"C'mon, baby, the next few days are going to be a blitz, let's relieve some tension."

"If I recall correctly," Viv chimed in as she shimmied out her trousers, "our tradition is to abstain from sex the week of Praksepana until I give you your pre-keynote blow job."

"Fuck tradition," Adam growled, unhooking her bra.

"Fuck me," Viv keened when he sank his teeth into the juncture of her shoulder.

Once they were both naked, Adam maneuvered Viv flush against the cool glass of their bedroom's ceiling to floor panes.

Despite being mesmerized by the city that glittered below her, Viv objected in a feeble whisper, "Someone will see."

"Want 'em to." "Exhibitionism? That's new."

Adam landed a slap across her ass. "Evolve or die, baby."

Then:

Necessity is the mother of invention, but Viv didn't invent Brahman's now billion-dollar proprietary AI because she needed to. The processes, the coding, the algorithms had all simply come to Viv her sophomore year of undergrad like a divine, digital download. Her ensuing years at Stanford were all about seeing if it was actually as implementable as she believed it could be.

It was. The Turing tests proved it, plus the fact it did all of Viv's post-grad coursework for her, which allowed Viv to focus on making it better. She knew created something that would change the world. She knew it. This had the potential to be the moon landing and discovery of fire combined.

What Viv seemingly needed was a male co-founder. A man she could trust. And since the only man she did trust, Raj, had rejected her, Viv decided to invent one. The AI created an email address for itself, doctored a few fake social media profiles, and hacked the Stanford website to add its new identity to the school's alumni directory in less than an hour.

So it was with a melting pint of Ben & Jerry's on her lap that Viv cold-emailed all of the VC's she met with from the new email address. For good measure she changed Minerva AI to Brahman Tech. All it took to give Viv the power to change her and everyone's lives was swapping the name in the signature from Vivika Burr to Adam Vateri.

Now:

Raj arrived at Viv's at the crack of dawn. He wasn't worried about intruding. Viv would be up. Dasa fired off a message to let Viv know he'd arrived once his Ratha car had parked itself. The last thing either of them wanted was to wake Minnie up with his entrance.

Viv ushered him inside their palatial, starkly modern penthouse without a word. "Where is he?"

She cocked her head toward Adam's office. He knew that she wouldn't go in with him. In the beginning, Viv had insisted on supervising when Raj worked on Adam. But that soon changed. Viv "couldn't see him like that" she claimed. It infuriated and concerned him equally.

"Just fix it." Viv would swear it was a plea, but all Raj heard was a demand. "If it happens again this week, we're fucked."

Raj wanted to snap that he was well aware, their shares were divided evenly after all, fuck-ups hurt him just as much as they did Viv. Instead, he nodded and let himself in.

Adam was working away at his computer as Raj gently closed the door behind him. "Hey man, next time can you knock or something if you're going to bar-"

Raj flicked his forehead and Adam collapsed over his keyboard. He lugged the other man upright in the chair and got to work.

Then:

Viv blamed internalized misogyny for why she hadn't thought it through. She'd gotten so many rejections, had been written off by so many smarmy VC assholes that she had begun to believe it would never happen. So when the emails, and requests for meetings, and competing offers began to roll in avalanche fashion, Viv was in shock.

Video calls had only worked for so long. It had been fun to design an avatar - what woman wouldn't want to create her ideal man? But when Sequoia told her that they wouldn't get a penny unless she and Adam did an investor dinner, Viv didn't have a choice.

She went to Raj with an offer he couldn't refuse: millions, generous equity, a CTO title, and legally binding paperwork that Dasa would be their first project. It was all well and good, but after a year of repetitive, corporate bullshit at AAB, it was the chance to build the prototype he'd been constructing in his head every night before he fell asleep that had convinced Raj to sign on.

Plus, it was for Viv. If he nailed this, maybe she'd finally see him as more than the sexless blob he'd been to her since undergrad orientation. Raj mechanically expounded on Viv's staggeringly brilliant algorithms to make her the "dick" she needed to change the world.

He was going to make her the best "dick" she, or anyone else for that matter, had ever seen.

And it worked. Adam was not only a conscious machine, but thanks to Raj and Viv's collective efforts, he was frighteningly human. Viv had achieved the motherfucking Singularity, but incomprehensibly to Raj, she demanded on keeping it a secret.

"Just until the deal closes," she'd told him, "then we'll tell them the truth about Adam. I feel like if we reveal anything now - Raj, their egos - they could walk."

By the time Raj realized that he'd perhaps done too good a job making Viv her dick, it was too late. His check had been cashed, his team hired, and his office decorated - hell, it was the day Raj put in an offer on his first house in Marin when the press release went out that Viv and Adam were engaged.

"What kind of crack did Lindsay have you smoke to agree to that?!" Viv recoiled. "It was my idea."

"He's not real, Viv." "He is-"

"No, he isn't-"

"Yes he is. He's conscious, so he's real." "Viv-"

"Besides, it makes sense. Everyone already assumes we're together. It'll be a great way to humanize the company, and if I'm really being honest, it's probably the best I can do."

"What the fuck does that mean?"

Viv dismissed him with a scoff and roll of her eyes. "You wouldn't understand." "Try me."

"Seriously, I don't want to talk about this with-"

"Humor me then. Seeing that I made your fiancé?"

"Fuck you."

"Sorry, you're right-"

"Fuck right off Raj."

And he did. Raj fucked off so hard he was Adam's best man at their godforsaken wedding.

Now:
"I think we should tell him."

Viv looked at him as if he'd suddenly sprouted a second head.

Raj faltered, "Don't you think he has a right to know?"

"You're joking," Viv declared with a stilted laugh and began making coffee, one of the few actions she refused to automate.

"I'm not."

"You have to be."

"The glitches are going to keep happening. The hardware can't keep up with how quickly his software is evolving. The brain we made can't store it, so he's basically been overloading himself."

"But you can fix it."

"Yeah, but we're going to have to do considerable work on how to expand his bandwidth without giving him a bigger head. Literally."

The coffee couldn't brew quickly enough. Viv labored a sigh, "Of all the fucking weeks-"

"That's why we need to tell him. It could happen during his keynote-"

"It better fucking not-"

"Viv if he knew, he could announce it himself - we'd break the internet. It would be the world-altering moment you've dreamt of."

Another heavy exhale from Viv, this one followed by a gulp of coffee. It wasn't her dream. Not anymore. It was Raj's. They'd had this debate countless times. "The world's not read-"

A "Mooooooooom" and the pitter patter of little feet provided Viv with a welcome distraction. Minerva was a sight for both of their weary eyes as she barrelled into view, still clad in her Paw Patrol pajamas. Viv scooped her up into her arms with an innately maternal fluidity that made Raj's heart shatter and swell all at once.

Part of their deal had included Raj getting naming rights for all the company's products and services in exchange for finishing Adam's body and keeping the truth a secret. So Viv had repurposed the name for what she'd believed to be her greatest creation when a creation far greater came along in the form of a fidgety and precocious daughter.

"Mommy, I want pancakes," Minnie declared, then immediately began wriggling out her mother's grasp when she spotted Raj.

"Come here Minnie Mouse," he accepted her with a bear hug. "Yeesh, you're getting big, beta."

"Daddy says I'm in the ninety-fourth person tiles-"

"Per-cent-ile," Viv gently corrected from where she whispered the pancake order to their Chef who'd since joined the fray.

"Per-cent-ile," Minnie parroted then pushed on, "for my height."

Raj *oooed* and *ahhhhed* as he was expected to, but the way Minnie had said "Daddy" echoed in his brain, the word bouncing endlessly around in his skull as he examined the child in his arms, then held her closer.

Yet Minnie didn't allow such a close embrace for long, "Uncle Raj! Pumme down!!"

When Raj left twenty minutes later, he texted Viv: If you don't tell him this week, I will.

Then:
The pair marvelled at the man before them in silence. Their work was done, all they had to do was to give him a jump. Mary Shelley would be rolling in her grave. Or would she be as impressed as Viv was? If she knew, would she go back and revise the book, changing Victor Frankenstein to Victoria? Or if Viv was really going to let herself daydream, Vivika?

Raj interrupted her reverie. "How do you feel?" "Relieved."

"We still have to do the Turing tests to make sure."

"He'll pass them." Viv had no doubt.

Raj didn't share in her confidence just yet. "You're sure?"

"Of course I am. I always knew we'd create something that would change the world." She grinned at him and in that moment, Raj knew exactly why he'd fallen in love with her.

Now:
Vivika Vateri was not the type to cower at a threat. But deep down, she knew he was right. It was just...Raj couldn't have picked a worse week to grow a conscience after seven years of well-compensated complacency.

The run up to Praksepana was more chaotic than usual this year with the introduction of a concrete, human version of Dasa in addition to the standard four new products they used the event to announce. She was so wrapped up with how the general public would receive the new incarnation of Dasa - their verbiage had to be perfect, the demo had to be perfect - Viv barely had the wherewithal to contemplate how she was going to reveal the truth about himself and their marriage to her husband, a far more intelligent being than the walking, talking Dasa they were going to peddle to the masses starting Friday.

And of course Raj had suddenly developed the inability to let things go. The morning of Praksepana during the load-in to Lincoln Center, Raj pulled Viv aside to commend her when Adam and Viv entered hand-in-hand.

"He's not threatening to hack and fry the energy grid, I'm impressed."

Viv's pursed lips and furrowed brow revealed her guilt wordlessly. Still, she shot at him, "You realize you put me in an impossible position."

"I can't do this anymore."

"Well I don't have a choice!! You can send me all the vague, threatening texts you want, but I'm the one who has to think this all through! Forget how he'll take it, people will riot in the fucking streets if we don't go about this in the right way, and we'll be in jail without a motherfucking paddle as our life's work burns around us. Did that ever fuckling occur to you?"

"Did if it ever fucking occur to you that he could shortcir-"

"I hate that word-"

Raj scoffed, then continued "-- he could zone out during today's keynote? We'll be even more fucked than we he did on national TV Monday."

"You won't be fucked, I'll be fucked. I'll lose my husband. Fuck, Minnie will be fucked.

How dare you do this to me when you know what it'll do to her?"

"Because if I hear her call me Uncle Raj one more time, I'll jump off the GW."

"You knew what you were signing up for," Viv countered. "We did this together, and I made sure you were taken care of.

Honestly, Minnie likes you more than me, that has to count for something, doesn't it?"

"We've gone too far."

"That may be true, but we can't take away our employees' livelihood because you want... I mean, I don't even know, you-"

"I love you."

A string of expletives detonated in Viv's mind. He'd finally said it. She knew, of course she knew, she'd known for years, but at last Raj had said it. Fuck. Her business, her marriage, her daughter had all been contingent on Raj never actually acting on his feelings for her.

"You don't love him, you love me."

Viv could understand why Raj wanted her love for himself, but he couldn't – or rather wouldn't want to understand why Viv wouldn't want to give up what she had with Adam. Besides, Raj couldn't actually love her after all she'd put him through. Viv struggled not to despise him in that moment, to not resent that she'd needed Raj in the first place.

"You're not making any sense. And I do love you, what we've made-"

"Cut the bullshit, Viv! He's me. I made him myself, but in the packaging of your choice."

Suddenly, the two thousand, five hundred, and eighty six seat theater became a claustrophobic prison to Viv. What she said next would decide her fate. She tried to soften her features, train them into the expression he wanted to see, instead of the truth of what she felt. Terror.

"I want to work this out." She meant it. "I really do. For your sake, for Minnie's, for Brahman's... and I promise I will tell Adam later. We can talk tonight, but you need to let me get through the next three hours."

Viv searched Raj's face for any evidence she'd convinced him. The sour, knotted pit in

Viv's stomach grew when was met with the same grim, tortured expression of consternation. It was a face that she watched shed the lingering baby fat of adolescence, brown skin that now bore ever-deepening lines across his forehead, in between his brows, and on the outer corners of his eyes. Whether it was from the stress of working with Viv or loving her, she couldn't be sure, but Viv knew she'd all but etched them there herself.

Then, she watched as a realization dawned upon his face. "You don't love me. Or him. Do you?"

Viv's lip trembled. "No, I-"

"Fuck, I'm no better than him. You've got a hand up both our asses, don't you?"

"Please, I am begging you-"

"I can-I won't do this anymore, Vivika. If you don't tell Adam today, I wi-"

"Tell me what?"

Viv's stomach turned to stone in the span of a second. Nevertheless, she whirled around to face Adam and immediately put distance between her and Raj. "That we think the moments where you zone out may be the sign of something serious. I didn't want to tell you, you have enough on your mind before the keynote, but Raj felt-"

"That you had the right to know."

Adam shrugged. "I mean, I figured. We'll deal with it together, but hun, you completely missed soundcheck."

"Fuck. Sorry."

Raj glowered in place as Adam ushered her away from him. Lindsay soon joined Viv's side, talking a million miles a minute about some inane shit. Her words washed over Viv as unintelligible garble as she mindlessly followed her publicist to wherever she was leading them to.

She took Adam's hand and cut Lindsay off mid-sentence. "You can't leave my side today, okay?"

"That's sweet babe, but not exactly doable."

"Well, it has to be." For years, Viv refused to be a diva. As one of the few female COO's in her industry, it was on her to create a new paradigm of feminine leadership. Not a woman convincingly doing what a man would do, but truly feminine leader. So Viv didn't raise her voice, she didn't throw tantrums, and she didn't surround herself with a bevy of hot, barely legal interns. But these were desperate times, and she figured she'd earned the right to play the diva for once. "I don't care what you have to do Lindsay, but he's not leaving my side today, okay? And no phones."

"Viv, I know you're the boss here, but that's unhinged-"

"I DON'T CARE!" Her protest filled the entirety of the David H. Koch Theater's expansive, gilded lobby. Viv recollected herself. "Raj is...he's gone off the deep end. He's not handling the risk of a poor reaction to Dasa today. So we need to be in lockstep and keep each other close, because he said some crazy shit to me just now."

Lindsay didn't have any reason not to believe Viv. "I'm on it, I'll make sure Kayla keeps an eye on him too."

Adam scrutinized her for a moment that felt like a century, then also fell into line.

Then:
"I love you, you know."

Viv froze. AI's had the tendency to profess love for their human counterparts rather quickly and out of nowhere, like Adam had just done.

"I don't think you even know what love is," she accused him, albeit playfully.

"Oh yeah?" Adam was undaunted by her dismissal. "Then explain to me why I want to be with you every day for the rest of eternity?"

"What if we stopped having sex?"

"This is more than sex and you know that. And before you say it – it's more than business too."

All Viv ever wanted to do was write algorithms and have a family. She arguably made the most sophisticated algorithm of all time, but she knew sharing it would cost Viv her imaginary future family. No matter how hard she tried to shrink and demure herself, men were always intimidated by her intelligence. If it wasn't her intelligence, it was her ambition. Viv couldn't blame them either. Who the hell wouldn't be emasculated by, as Raj had once so eloquently put it, the creator of the motherfucking Singularity?

But Adam wasn't intimidated or emasculated by her. Nor did he want to be her kept man either. And sure, she'd programmed him to be a good feminist, but love? Viv had figured he wasn't capable. It was what had kept them as two separate entities. The human and the machine. Yet why wouldn't Adam be capable of love? Other than being made of completely organic matter, he met every definition of a conscious being.

"I...I don't know what to say," she stammered.

"I'm told 'I love you too' is customary."

"More than you'll ever know."

Now:

Her incredibly practical, intricate, and mature plan of keepaway worked for most of the day. But Praksepana was a blitz, and even despite the whole of Brahman's publicity team's best efforts, Viv and Adam were separated.

"WHERE IS HE?" she demanded as Lindsay tried to corral her irate boss into her dressing room. Viv had left mid-interview with Wired as soon as she'd realized Adam was missing.

Lindsay wrangled Viv inside only to find that Adam was already in the dressing room waiting for her. Viv's entire countenance changed at the sight of him.

"Get out," she whispered to Lindsay and the entourage of assistants and junior publicists.

"Sorry, Lindsay, everyone." In stark contrast to his wife, Adam was calm. "I need to speak to Vivika alone."

The room swam. He definitely knew. Viv's breaths came in pants. Raj was a dead man.

Still, she hoped against hope. "You here for your pre-keynote blowie?"

"Right, because I'm your sentient vibrator."

"No, you're my husband, who I love more than words, and whatever he told you-"

"He told me the truth."

"His truth. Don't you think I deserve to tell you mine?"

"You must have programmed me to not think about it too much - why I never go to the doctor, why I can only eat that stupid smoothie, it all makes perfect sense if I'd been permitted to put one iota of thought into-" Adam stopped himself. "Who's Minnie's father?"

"Adam, you are."

"Who is Minerva's biological father?"

"You've raised her-"

"You're a monster!" he spat at her. "Sure, I'm in the midst of an existential crisis, but I can't imagine-or rather, compute-how it's been for him?! Having to watch me play house with his kid!!"

"God, it's inescapable, the bro code transcends all," Viv collapsed on the couch that regularly housed some prima ballerina. "I didn't want the fame, the renown, the power, I just wanted to share what I created with the world-"

"Really? Because you're famous, renowned, and powerful-"

"AND I WORK FOR YOU!!" Her outburst silenced him. "Imagi—sorry, compute what you think this would've looked like if our genders were reversed. The first sentient machine would've been a glorified sex doll who would've quickly lost her glory once she became one of many in an all-AI harem. Adam, I kept it from you because I wanted you to feel as human as possible. I wanted to marry you, I wanted you to experience fatherhood, I want us to be partners because I respect you."

"This isn't respect. This is the sickest game of dolls in the history of humankind."

"Did he tell you that every single VC I pitched Miner-Brahman to rejected me? I had created the best AI that Stanford had ever seen but no one off-campus took me seriously. Not even Raj. I begged him to come on as co-founder and he said no. It wasn't until I had created you and there was money on the table he agreed to help me. I didn't want to create you, Adam. I wish you were some guy I met at a friend's birthday on the Embarcadero, but that's not what happened. I had to."

"You didn't 'have to'--"

"Oh, yes I did! Our enemies were just as close to machine consciousness as I was! This was the only way! The reason no one knows we did it first beside me and Raj and the fucking president is because I wanted to prevent unrest. Raj agreed to ease the populace into this level of artificial intelligence. I wanted to nip societal unease in the bud and be the leader of a peaceful, productive-"

"STOP LYING TO ME!" Viv feared his anger would short circuit him, but Adam continued undeterred, "I know you, and that's not why you did this. You didn't need to marry me or tell me I was the father of your kid. You could've told me from the start. We could've been colleagues."

Viv's lip trembled again, "You're the most intelligent AI on the planet, but there are still things you don't understand. Chiefly, what it is like to be a woman in a male-dominated field – scratch that, just to be a woman period. Men wouldn't care about how rich or influential I'd become because they didn't like how smart I was. I couldn't be the CEO of my own goddamn company."

"You're right, I'll never understand it," Adam admitted, "but it doesn't excuse your actions."

"You're not going to stay on script during your keynote, are you?"

A knock at the door prevented Adam from answering. Lindsay's voice urged from the other side, "Guys, I am so sorry, but we've held the room for the past fifteen minutes. Is there any way you can put a pin in this until after the presentation?"

"One more minute, okay?" Viv stared straight into Adam's eyes, the spellbinding hazel hue she'd chosen herself. "I know you're angry and you feel betrayed, but I do love you. I always have."

"I hate you."

Viv nodded, a wordless concession that hey, she'd set herself up for that. "If I were you, I wouldn't get too hung up on my biology, because that was a pretty fucking human response."

It took one breath for Vivika to compose herself after her world fell apart. Her face was a blank mask when she emerged from the dressing room.

Raj caught a glimpse of her as she was getting mic'd. Viv always took the stage before Adam at Praksepana. Her "presentation" didn't present much of anything other than Adam. She was essentially an opening act they trotted out for "girl power" before the main event. This year would be different. When Viv's eyes landed on Raj, they bore through him as if he wasn't there.

As far as she was concerned, he wasn't.

Thunderous applause greeted Viv when she stepped on stage, a grin now painted onto her mask.

"Thank you all," she began, her voice more robust and sonorous since she knew to use her diaphragm when addressing a crowd. "Before I introduce our CEO, there's a few things I, Vivika Burr Vateri, need to address. Not only as the COO of Brahman Tech but as a human who identifies as a woman. The year I developed the artificial intelligence that all of Brahman products utilize -- and yes it was me, and me alone, who created it - 1.9 percent of venture capital funding went to female-led start-ups in this country. Not even two percent."

The room broke out into indignant whispers and groans.

"I pitched twenty seven venture capital firms with glowing recommendations from the most tenured and respected minds at Stanford. Every single VC rejected me. Usually without much reason or feedback. To be fair, I did get one offer for funding, but I had to give the guy a blowjob for it."

The indignant whispers and groans raised a decibel in volume and became more appropriately more scandalized.

"Funnily enough, the percentage of female-founded startups increased to a whopping 17.2 percent if there was a man on the management team. Now, imagine you're me. You know you've created something that will not only change the world, but change it for the better. And you all do feel like Brahman's products have made your life better, yes? At the very least, easier?"

Viv paused for the whoops and applause and then went on.

"But no one will give you a chance, not even your best friend. So I did something radical.

Something that had never been done before. Something in a moral gray area, but you know what? I've spent every single fucking day since then trying to take care of the people who that choice affected, because not only does it affect all of you, it affects those closest to me. It affects my four-year-old daughter whose life I know I am about to ruin because I've been forced to tell you this before I was ready."

The theater fell silent. Viv could hear a pin drop from the rafters from the stage.

"I achieved machine consciousness seven years ago. There has been a sentient AI living amongst us since then and it's none other than my husband, the CEO of Brahman Technologies, Adam Vateri. The room exploded into shouts, gasps, and general uproar, but Viv pushed on anyway, "Honey, why don't you come on out and properly introduce yourself?"

And it was as Adam staggered onto the stage in front of an audience that had descended into pandemonium, Vivika strolled out of the theater.

EASY PREY

Terry Sanville

Heading east on Interstate 10, Matt watched the dashed lane-lines fly by the produce truck, its headlights barely making a dent in the darkness.

"I can drop you at the exit," Emilio said. "But you sure you don't wanna go into Tonopah? It's gonna get cold out there, below freezing."

"Thanks but no. I've got to get east. I'm supposed to meet someone in Dallas in a couple days and they won't wait."

Matt smiled to himself. He didn't know anybody in Dallas and he'd probably try crossing the border at El Paso. They shouldn't be looking for him there.

Emilio clicked on the truck's ancient AM radio and dialed in a Latino station, the signal full of static. "Dallas, that's a long way, man. You'd better get yourself a waterproof jacket. It's gonna rain like hell."

"Don't care. I just need to get there."

"But tonight . . . you gonna sleep out on the desert?"

"If I have to."

"Don't. You'll freeze."

"Thanks for the tip. Wake me when we get to Tonopah."

"Sure, buddy, sure."

Matt slumped in the seat, pulled the brim of his cap down to keep the glare from oncoming headlights out of his eyes, and fell asleep. In what felt like only a few minutes the driver shook him awake.

"We're here, buddy." Emilio pointed to the Exxon station, convenience store and truck stop next to the off-ramp. "They've got coffee in the store. But they close at midnight."

"Thanks for the ride." Matt cranked the ancient handle and climbed out, slamming the door with a hollow metallic crash. Smoking, the truck turned south toward the few scattered buildings and a 1950s-style motel, its parking lot empty.

He stood at the mouth of the Interstate's onramp, his jacket zipped tight and collar turned up. A frigid wind blew strands of shoulder-length hair back in his face. He stuffed it inside his jacket and stomped the ground, trying to keep the feeling in his feet. A few semis passed him on their way to Phoenix and points east. But traffic died, the truck stop quieted, occupied by only a few long-haul rigs overnighting in the back parking area. *This is stupid,* he thought. *Nobody's gonna give me a ride this time of night. This whole thing is nuts.*

Matt thought back over the afternoon's events. He'd cased the Beverly Hills house for two weeks, knew when the husband and wife came home from work. Knew when the nanny left to take the kids to school and returned with them in mid-afternoon. Knew when the housekeeper arrived and departed. Knew everything about them. It should have been easy, easy pickin's.

Break in, disarm the alarm, ransack the joint at his leisure, then fence whatever he could carry away and use any cash to buy a steak dinner, some coke and the best bottle of single-malt scotch he could find and share it with a hooker after screwing her brains out.

But the whole deal had gone south when the couple came home early, found him on the sofa watching TV and drinking some of their fancy imported beer. The giant husband charged, looking to tear him to pieces. Matt pulled his piece and dropped him with two quick shots to the chest. The wife screamed and screamed and screamed, wouldn't shut up. Matt shut her up with a blast to the head. It happened quickly. Even with all the ruckus and mess - they had white carpets - Matt had stayed calm.

The TV continued to mutter in the background. Matt listened. The neighborhood dogs stayed quiet. The huge houses along the street stood mostly empty - everybody away making those big bucks. Matt left the mark's house and casually loaded the van with loot, taking his time, out of sight from the street. It would have been a clean getaway except the place had security cameras. Then his van crapped out before he could get on the Interstate. He stuffed the jewelry and cash in his pockets and ditched the van on a back street before catching a ride with Emilio.

Matt thought about what had gone wrong, what he should have done differently, would do differently the next time. Maybe the ski mask hadn't hidden his identity enough? *Should have checked the damn van before using it or stolen something better. This is totally stupid.*

The lights at the convenience store flickered then went dark. The cockroach motel looked locked up tight or maybe even abandoned. Matt turned north, walked under the freeway bridge and headed into open desert along an asphalt road. The wind died and the cold seeped into his bones. Light traffic on the Interstate barely whispered. Across the desert plain a light flickered. He turned onto a dirt track. The mysterious light drew him onward, stumbling over rocks and roots in the night.

As he approached, fuzzy images resolved into a campfire next to a huge camper with its levelers and awning in place, as if it had been there a while. An old man grasping a glass sat next to the fire. A rifle lay across his lap. Matt shoved a hand in the pocket that held his pistol and fingered its familiar grip.

"If you're a crook, you're a stupid one," the old guy called. "You're making enough noise to scare away the scorpions."

"I didn't mean to disturb you," Matt said and approached slowly while slipping the pistol's safety off.

The old guy laid a hand on his rifle. "What the hell you doing out here?"

"I got stuck at the exit. Nothing's going on. The market shut down and—"

"You're freezing your ass off." The old guy chuckled. "Come near the fire. Here, drink this." He handed Matt the glass of booze, his other hand never leaving the rifle.

"Thanks. I was hoping I could hitch a ride east from some trucker at the Exxon."

"Not this late. My name's George by the way."

"I'm . . . I'm Nate."

"You don't sound sure of that."

"Just cold, that's all."

George disappeared into the camper and returned with a lawn chair. The two sat as close as possible to the crackling fire, the burning creosote bush sending out a strong, almost toxic odor.

"You want more?" George asked and retrieved a square unlabeled bottle from next to his chair.

"Yeah. Whoa, that's enough."

"So why you out here in the middle of the night, in the middle of nowhere?" George asked.

"My car blew up. I'm trying to get to Dallas to meet a friend."

George whistled. "That's a long way."

"Don't I know it. I figured I'd bum rides from truckers."

"Good luck with that. I'm surprised that truck stop stays open. Santiago and his wife manage the place, work for Pilot. They're barely scraping by and the corporation must be propping that place up."

The fire warmed Matt, the booze loosened his muscles and his mouth. "So why are *you* out here?"

"I'm from Seattle. I leave when it starts raining and come here. Like the quiet. I'm far enough from the highway that my old ears don't hear the noise."

"But doesn't the heat and cold get to you? This place must cook during the day."

George laughed. "Yeah, some folks say my brain is fully baked. But I still got some smarts – like I know that bulge in your jacket pocket isn't your Gideon's Bible."

Matt smiled. "So that's why you keep ahold of that deer rifle."

"Can't be too careful. The trick is to not let it harden you. I avoid becoming a jerk by avoiding people. But I still try . . . to be kind, ya know, when I do meet them."

Matt took another swallow of booze and leaned back in his chair. "Good for you. I'm afraid I see people differently. They're either trying to take me down or they're my prey."

George leaned forward. "Prey?"

"Yeah, you know, like a gazelle being chased by a lion."

"That sounds brutal, like words from a . . . what do they call 'em . . . a sociopath."

Matt threw his head and shoulders back and laughed, almost tipping the chair over. "That's me, George, that's me." He noticed that the old man's grip on the rifle tightened.

"Did you always want to be a game hunter?"

"Don't really know. I just grew into it and nobody could show me anything better."

"Really?" George asked. "You never had anybody show you a different way of thinking . . . a less brutal way?"

"I've always done my own thinking."

"Huh. So . . . so when was the last time you went after prey?" George murmured.

"This afternoon."

"So you're runnin' from the . . . the game wardens."

"Yeah."

"I won't tell anybody. But you know, you'll eventually become prey yourself."

"Yeah, so?"

"That's a hard life, don't you think?"

"Sure, but sometimes it's good. You shoulda seen the sexy gal I was with last night."

"But it's not good now, is it? "

"No, not now."

George poured more booze into Matt's glass from the square bottle. It had a strange metallic aftertaste but properly kicked his ass. Matt tossed it down.

"You like my booze?" George asked.

"Yeah, it's kinda strange, but . . . "

"I make it myself from saguaro cactus and my own special ingredients. But watch it. Drink too much and it'll take you to a place you won't like."

"Most booze does." Matt offered his glass for another double shot.

George handed him the half-full bottle. "Take it and enjoy. I'm gonna turn in. I'll bring you a couple blankets and you can sleep by the fire." He retrieved two worn Army blankets from the camper and handed them to Matt. "Be sure to shake your covers in the morning and keep your shoes on. The snakes and scorpions like to hide there overnight."

"Thanks for the tip."

The camper door crunched shut behind George followed by a rattle of chains and locks. Matt threw more wood on the fire, wrapped the blankets around himself and leaned back in the rickety lawn chair. He sipped his drink, then took swigs directly from the bottle. A golden moon the size of a pizza hung low in the night sky. Matt smiled to himself. *In the morning I'll be on my way to Mexico . . . go down to Cancun and lie on a beach, plenty of rich tourists to prey on. My life will be good again. I'll let George skate – lucky for him he doesn't have anything I want, except maybe the recipe for his fake tequila.*

Matt took a final swig from the bottle and let it slip to the ground. He inhaled the pungent odors from the fire. Without warning, blackness closed in.

A white-hot sun woke him. Matt stared upward into a dusty yellow sky. The air smelled different, free of vehicle exhaust. *Probably just the booze messing with my senses* he thought. He rubbed his eyes and pushed himself up. *What the fuck!* George's camper, the fire pit and everything he remembered from the night before had disappeared.

Matt turned in a circle and stared across a vast plain covered in knee-high grass and studded with strange-looking trees and shrubs. In the distance something loud and angry trumpeted, raising clouds of dust. A herd of weird-looking cattle mixed in with zebras grazed nearby. They seemed oblivious to his presence. ZEBRAS!

Matt again scanned the plain, looking for the Interstate and the Exxon station. They too had disappeared. A herd of gazelles with long pointed horns rocketed past. Off to his right a low guttural growl almost stopped his heart. He turned and watched a pride of lions advance, the shaggy-maned males holding back, yawning, the sleek females focused on the kill, their amber eyes glowing, lips quivering.

Matt fumbled in his pocket for the pistol, the fear turning him cold. But the first lioness toppled him, her jaws closing on his neck and jugular. A thunder of pain and the light faded. The lions had found easy prey.

THAT THING WE KILLED

Wayne Kyle Spitzer

I still don't know what it was, that thing we killed. I've seen things like it, in movies and on TV. But those things were made up, or based on the bones of extinct animals. Like monsters. This wasn't like that. This was just an animal, though not one that any of us had ever seen. Not in Halcomb County, that's for sure.

It hadn't threatened us, as far as I can remember. It turned on us, hissing kind of, a limp trout falling from its mouth, because we had startled it. I sure remember that mouth, opened like a wet, black rosebud, showing spiny teeth, a white palate. Maybe it had lunged toward us. Maybe it deserved what it got. I don't even remember who fired first or why. It was a long time ago and everyone involved is dead, except me.

We'd gone out that day to get a trophy for my thirteenth birthday, even though it wasn't hunting season. We made an odd sort of family back then: Uncle Horseshoe (because of his mustache), Hank, and Frank Garstole, who lived in a cabin next door. Uncle Horseshoe owned every kind of gun imaginable, from Scout rifles to muskets, and the walls of his house were covered with every kind of trophy, the great prize being a seventine rack of moose over the fireplace, which he said he'd killed alone in the Blue Mountains in December of '62, but which Frank said he stole from a woodpile in Alaska.

Frank laughed at the thought of us going out. "Horseshoe," he said, "Now what do you think a game warden's gonna say when he sees you outfitted like brigands?"

I remember Horseshoe just staring at him—he was huge on staring. "Don't worry about it, Frank," he said.

Frank said to me after they'd gone out, "They're scarin' up their own trouble, boy. Let 'em go."

But I ran after them.

We startled it, as I've said.

We were rounding a deadfall, bitching about how it had been a wasted day, when we saw it. I saw it complete for only an instant; it looked like a snake—not a Rattler or a Moccasin, more like a Python, or one of those Boas you sometimes see in National Geographic, with its giant body held up by an entire hunting party—a snake threaded through a turtle. But then it fled, hissing kind of, slinking back into the water and paddling away, toward the center of the lake.

I wasn't frightened by it. It didn't look or act like The Giant Behemoth, or Reptilicus, or anything else you might see at a matinee or in comic books. It was just an animal, though not one any of us had ever seen. But then bullets went punching through its blubber. Then the thing's blood went spraying in all directions.

There was a rickety dock nearby, which we used to get closer. I remember the spent shells dropping and plinking off its boards. The thing turned on us; I suppose it had to. It tried to hiss but managed only a choked gargle. Blood bubbled from its throat and spilled from its mouth.

"Take the fatal shot," said Horseshoe. He must have laid down his rifle because I remember him helping to steady my own. "Easy now, you'll own this forever—" I stared the thing in the eye and squeezed the trigger.

It threw back its head, rising up. It gasped for breath, spitting more blood. It barked at the sky. Then it fell, head thumping against the deck. Its serpentine neck slumped. The rest of its blood spread over the boards and rolled around our boots and flowed between the planks.

I was the first to step forward, looking down at the thing through drifting smoke.

Its remaining eye seemed to look right back. I got down on my knees to look closer. The thing exhaled, causing the breathing holes at the top of its head, behind its eyes, to bubble. I waited for it to inhale, staring into its eye—I could see myself there as well as the others, could see the sky and the scattered clouds. The whole world seemed contained in that moist little ball. Then the eye rolled around white—it shrunk, drying, and the thing's neck constricted. And it died.

Horseshoe slapped my back, massaged my neck. "How's it feel, little buddy?"

But I didn't know what I felt. I could only stare at the eye, now empty.

We went back the next day with Frank Garstole and a bunch of others with the intent of hoisting it out of the lake, but there had been a thunderstorm and whatever it was we had killed was gone, slipped back into the water, I suppose. Old Frank sure had a laugh about that, chiding Horseshoe, "Well, the bigger they are the more apt they are to get away."

Horseshoe just stared, like he might kill him right there on the spot. It was the same look he gave me when, visiting years later, I joked about that rack of moose he'd found in Alaska.

We'd been sitting on his back porch, which was falling to ruin just like his body, having beers, and—well, it was a look that said it was time to go. I went and never saw him again.

I still think about that thing we killed, from time to time. Sometimes I dream about it. Sometimes in the dreams I am in the water with the thing, where it kills me rather than me killing it. Sometimes, as I sink, I see it hovering high above. I see it through a cloud of blood and a ceiling of water, rimmed in solar fire, beautiful. Other times I am the thing, and I rise, spitting blood, barking at the sky.

GATE K22

John Stadelman

His life was perfect now. Except for when he heard things.
Ian.
"What?"
Anita looked up from her phone. "Huh? Again?"
Ian closed his eyes, rubbing his forehead. "Yeah. Sorry, babe."
She put a hand on the back of his neck, massaged it. "It's okay."
"Next time I hear it, I'm just gonna shout, 'What!'"
"Don't do that." She grinned. "That's crazy."
They were sitting at their gate, waiting for the flight that would take them to Rome. After wanting this kind of trip for so long, it was finally happening: backpacking from Italy up into the Alps, then on to Paris. It was their first time out of the country—

like him, Anita grew up too poor for vacations, so she burned with the desire to travel, to get lost in the world. In the past year they'd gone to both coasts and the cities and countrysides in between. For this trip, they'd each picked a language—French for Ian, Italian for Anita—to learn as deeply as possible in six months, with enough German between them to get through the Alps.

The bustle of O'Hare on a July afternoon, all the families and lone travelers hauling rolling bags, running to their connecting flights, not a mask in sight because they were no longer needed. Ian was overcome by that feeling of disbelief, that this was his life. This wonderful life.

"Look, isn't that adorable?" Anita held up her phone, showing him a photo that Joel had sent of his two-year-old daughter napping on the couch with Rufus, Ian and Anita's Rhodeisan Ridgeback.

Ian smiled. "He won't even miss us." They'd gotten Rufus from a shelter as a joint Christmas present. Like Ian, Anita wanted to get an older one because they weren't adopted as often. A pang hit him, missing Rufus hard for a moment—but it passed, as he reminded himself that he was about to travel abroad in the summer with the love of his life. With Anita, who'd come out of nowhere, as lonely and resigned as him that evening at an anonymous bar, needing someone to love her and to love back. Anita, who was self-possessed, funny, incredibly smart, down as much for a night out as she was for a night in. And who was beautiful, her smile in the winter from above a scarf like a summation of everything he wanted in life, rivaled only by her smile in the summer from below her sunglasses. Whose finger, he hoped, would be wearing the ring hidden in his bag that he'd produce when they reached her most anticipated stop in Rome, the Trevi Fountain.

Anxious at that thought, he had to stand, but covered it up as a stretch. "I'm gonna get a coffee. Want anything?"

"Nope. I'll hold down our position."

"Roger roger."

"Hurry up, though. Boarding starts soon."

In line at the nearest Starbucks, Ian reminded himself that his nervousness at proposing was generalized. They were perfect together, no red flags, just one or two orange ones and everybody had those. They'd shown as much of themselves to each other as was possible, really, in a way that Ian had never felt or known he could feel. She'd told him the same. And agreed that he'd materialized into her life the same way she had for him: from the cold depths of a creeping, personal apocalypse, furtively watching him in the bar mirror and looking the way he'd felt.

This is your life now, he told himself. *It's okay for it to be good.*

Something was beeping, just teeny enough to be annoying. One of those little cars they used to shuttle people around? Passive alarm for a door that shouldn't be open? The simple *beep... beep* of it was familiar, but he couldn't place it. He closed his eyes for a moment.

... up.

The word stretched out, echoing through his mind. It was a fragment of the phrase he'd been trying to make out from that recurring dream, the one he couldn't remember when he woke up. His head hurt.

When reached the counter the barista spoke, mouth moving, but he didn't hear her.

"Sorry, what?"

Mouth moving, the obvious question: *What can I get you?*

"Um... tall coffee." And he made it through the transaction without hearing a word she said. Heading back for the gate— K22, he reminded himself—he passed a family arguing with each other in complete silence. A gate agent said nothing into a microphone to the thick semi-circle of passengers. Just shoes on the floor, the drone of rolling bags, clothes rustling.

beep ... beep

Flicker of dark movement in his periphery. He looked, and the shadow disappeared.

Back at the gate, Anita asked, "What's wrong?"

Out through the window, the July sunlight had dampened. The massive Boeing connected to their gate by the jet-bridge didn't gleam with the promise of another continent, but squatted like an old insect, decrepit and questionable.

"Hey?" She touched his arm. Worry on her face, in her eyes. "Ian?"

Ian.

"You're the only one I can hear," he said. "Why can I only hear you?"

Shadows flickered. He looked, and they disappeared.

Ian rubbed his forehead again, closing his eyes. "I need a nap."

Anita pulled his hand down and held it. "Just drink your coffee. Stay awake."

"Okay." He sipped it, relished the burn it left on his tongue.

It seemed darker down the length of the wide, peopled concourse. The lights had gone out, heavy darkness way down at gate K1.

He looked into Anita's eyes. "Just talk to me."

"About what?"

"About anything. I need to hear your voice."

She smiled—that magnificent smile—and stroked his cheek. "Well... in a few hours we're going to be in Rome. Pleasant weather, good wine, a lot of history. We'll see the Colosseum, the Pantheon, and of course the Trevi."

Farther down the concourse, more lights had gone out. Gate K8 disappeared.

"Then there's the Alps," Anita said. "And then we'll be in Paris. City of love."

"Don't get your hopes up, remember what Joel and Hailey said about it."

Her smile hadn't left, yet it seemed like it returned. "I don't care what they said. It's going to be amazing, know why?"

"Why?"

Ian.

"Because I'll be there with you."

beep ... beep

He started to close his eyes and she squeezed his hand. "I need you to stay awake, okay?"

"Okay. Why?"

"Because if you fall asleep here, you'll wake up out there. And we'll all die."

II

Ian's head shattered for a moment, then pulled back in. The silence stood complete, weighted by the darkening sky. He wasn't sure he'd heard her right.

"Just stay with me," she said. "We'll get on the plane, and in no time we'll be in Rome. I have a feeling it'll be a quick flight."

"No." He stood. "Something's happening to me. I need..."

He became aware of a new sound. It rose from the darkened end of the concourse, rising as the lights went out. A gnawing tumult, grinding forth from the flooding void whose source he didn't want to meet, even though he didn't know why.

Everyone was staring at him.

Gate agents, security guards, passengers. Nobody rushing to their flight, or talking on their phone, or ringing up orders at Starbucks.

And the sun was gone. The tarmac river-delta of runways beyond the windows stood motionless, taxiing planes frozen to the ground, the tiny forms of luggage handlers standing as safety-vest dots, staring across the flatness toward the terminal.

Gate K10 disappeared.

He swallowed, looked at his one anchor: Anita.

The gloom over her face, a reminder of the severe loneliness he'd seen in her eyes when they'd met at a bar, two years ago. Gloom that he'd watched dissipate as they grew closer, like morning mist burned away by afternoon sun as her life improved alongside his. But that shroud had fallen again, and he was standing in the airport with a stranger.

"You need to stay with me." Mounting panic in her voice. The expressions on the other people's faces carried that same hurt, and loneliness, and desperation.

The grinding cacophony in the dark.

"Where else would I go?"

"Back to the hell you escaped."

Gate K13 went dark.

He closed his eyes.

And opened them in the bar.

A frigid Tuesday evening in January. Barely tipsy, not even wanting to be here, but it was better than his shitty apartment. He couldn't handle that place, not when the night came. Not after having spent all day there, working from home. But nobody had time or energy to hang out... or maybe they didn't want to hang out with *him*. So what could he do with these empty nights? All the new hobbies he tried fell out with the winter malaise, which was glomped onto the pandemic malaise. He'd kept trying Bumble, but the dates were boring and strained. He wondered if his friends really were just too tired—that other great resignation—or if everyone had just decided to cut him loose. But not in one grand secret meeting; instead, and far worse, they all decided on their own that he wasn't that much fun, that he was in fact toxic no matter how much he worked on himself, that he was a tool to be used for support, entertainment and distraction. Beyond that, just an annoyance, a burden.

None of which was true. But he couldn't help feeling it.

And so here he sat, this bar like any other one, staving it off in Schlitz-laden anonymity. Feeling like taking up just this one stool was stealing too much from the world.

A woman sat a little ways down, and she was beautiful. A sort of presence around her, a power—but dampened by the sadness in her eyes. Was she glancing at him? Smiling a little, even? Or just at the empty spaces around him, the art on the walls?

Everything in him told him not to try. Then he stood, ignoring the clangor that sounded from the street. He prepared himself for coming across as off-putting—a burden—and then finding a quick way to break off, to leave the poor woman alone.

The clangor from the street rose into grinding cacophony.

"Hi."

She smiled, just a bit. "Hi."

"It's empty in here tonight, mind if I join you?"

She smiled a bit more, and with it emerged some more of that presence. She indicated the stool next to her. "Sure."

He sat. The door smashed open and the grinding crescendoed into screeching as clawed phantoms razored through screaming patrons.

He closed his eyes.

And opened them to his sister's wedding, standing as a groomsman with her and her partner's friends. Anita sat a row back from the front, her smile, she was so gorgeous. He wondered if she pictured herself up there, in as resplendent a dress as Nadine's... and standing across from Ian.

Nadine herself *was* resplendent in her dress, a powerful rejuvenation in her eyes as she held hands with her partner. She was a year sober, her arms free of track-marks, and no longer the miserable, depressed woman whose parents had insisted on still calling *Jason,* who hadn't known how hard Ian fought them for her. A year after the worst of it, their parents had finally accepted it, more completely than could have been hoped for—a miracle.

They themselves were doing so much better, too. Sitting in the front row of this church, tears in their eyes for the daughter they'd finally accepted as a daughter. And holding hands, having pushed through what would turn out to be their last separation, their last rough patch.

From the back rose a tide of grinding darkness. It flooded over the rows, mauling friends and family with such rapid efficiency that those in front didn't know until they themselves were shorn apart.

It touched Anita.

He blinked.

Joel, his best friend and business partner, was out of chemo. Though a month later he was right back in the hospital, this time rushing his wife, Hailey, in to give birth to their daughter. Ian stood with him after, watching the little bundle among the rows of them in the nursery. He heard the shadows moving through the hospital. A doctor stumbled around the corner, falling against the wall, shoes skidding out from under him. His eyes above his surgical mask pleaded to Ian. A clawed arm shot around the corner and pulled his head from his body.

Ian opened his eyes in the bookstore that he owned with Joel. The lighting was low, nighttime outside, just citylight through the shop windows. Anita stood under a *Grand Opening!* banner.

She smiled at him—tenuous, uncertain. She wasn't wearing the dress she'd had on at the opening, instead it was the shorts and jacket from the airport. Why had they been at an airport?

"Because we're going to Rome," she said.

She took a step toward him. He took one back, then his head blasted into pieces for a moment before pulling back in. Shadows darted out from the spaces between those shards and flitted along the ceiling, grainy, flexing serrated and thirsting claws.

Ian grabbed onto the front counter for support. "What's happening to me?"

"You're... struggling to keep it all together."

"Keep *what* together? My grip on reality?"

"Reality?" Anita said. She watched the shadows. "What is that, really? The physical world? It exists, but we experience it partially—we can only hear certain pitches, only see a portion of the light spectrum. We don't observe stars, just their ghost-images."

"I know all this."

"Of course you do. I know it, too... because you do."

"What does that mean?"

She ignored the question, continued on like he hadn't asked it. "There's the objective physical reality beyond us, and then there's our *individual* one. It's the fraction of the world that we can see, and smell, and hear—contained inside of us."

The bookshelves were gone, the neat aisles now a singular emptiness between four blank walls that had held a neighborhood message board and fliers for readings and bookclub meetings. It had regressed back to the empty storefront that he and Joel had leased on a loan, after his chemo went into remission. After he met Anita.

The shadows dived in a fluttering riot, but didn't touch him. He felt that they wanted to—but couldn't. Not yet.

"We each make our own reality," Anita said. "We sculpt it around the fractions of the external, physical world that we can't change. That's our world. And when our lives are good, our world seems brighter, brilliant... and worth it. When it's bad, we escape it with drinking, or drugs, or sex, anything to feel the rush—which is really just flirting with self-destruction. But what happens when that's not enough?"

Like the bookstore, she'd regressed: her face no longer willing to spring into an easy smile, her eyes sad in the winter night, the power in her crushed down.

He said, "You make it better."

"But when you *can't?* Like your life, before we met?"

"I don't want to think about that." But he couldn't help it. He'd been broke, stuck in a moldy basement apartment with deadbeat roommates and sketchy neighbors. Joel had been in chemo and Hailey dealt with it by drinking. Ian's arm was in a cast and even when it was taken out it ached all the time, but the doctor said he was fine and his prescription had run out so he was buying oxys from the sketchy neighbors because it was either that or drink through the pain like Hailey or blow his brains out.

You couldn't relax when your bones throbbed with every movement or lack of it. And what motivation he had for finding a way out—which seemed less and less possible as the pandemic exacerbated everything in the country and the world that made being poor a crime—fell away with every person who died, every friend who went conservative and broke his heart, every sleepless night aware of his solitary body in this basement mausoleum... no, not a mausoleum, he'd never be able to afford a burial that fancy. Not even wanting sex, just a body to curl up with, someone to hold. But he'd come to feel like a burden, unhelpful, just in the way. So he couldn't open up. Couldn't help anyone who needed it. All he *could* do was be in the way.

The Great Resignation was the trendy term being used to blame employees for knowing their worth, but Ian found another definition: the great resignation of caring, about oneself or, as much as one tried, about others. Or about a world that wasn't ending with either a bang or whisper, but with silence: the silence of phone calls that weren't made, of unsent texts. Visits canceled, plans forgotten, why bother reaching out to someone you haven't seen in a long time since it's all fucked and they probably don't care, justifiably, one way or the other if they hear from you or not? Why like a post, why comment on one, they won't care if you do or not. Or maybe they do. But still, what point?

That had been his reality. Fractional or not.

Anita touched his face. "That's what pushed you here, Ian. You couldn't do anything to help the people you love, and couldn't help yourself. And the world was falling apart, remember? What could you do then, except choose to watch it happen or block it out? When there was no way to make it better, no way out, what were you..." She closed her eyes. "What were you thinking about doing? To escape?"

He'd never told anyone, not even her, but in the depths of that time, he'd begun weighing the pros and cons of suicide with a detached intellectualism that scared him... but not enough to stop the thoughts. Or the preliminary planning.

"Instead," Anita said, "you found another way."

The shadows conjoined into a globulous mass and swooped down as one, and this time they touched him—but instead of tearing him apart, they reentered him. Like returning home.

Complete, uncompromising darkness.

Winter cold. The crummy radiator clanged, and his nose was infected by the reek of mildew and roommates' weed. This was the basement apartment.

He sheltered under layers of blankets, a fossil in strata clinging to his own body-warmth, which was all that was available in this miserable, callous existence that he called his life. He missed another body against his, just snuggling, holding him and being held by him, that silent affirmation of: *Us.*

On this night, he'd forgone the oxys and going out to a bar alone, instead trying for a sober sleep. His first in months. But his mind wouldn't stop racing through the hell of the wider world and his personal one, couldn't stop circling the untethered landscape over which he floated, not yet ghostly, but approaching it.

In that darkness his imagination began working, creating an undefined presence of warmth, of other, settling into the empty space between his arms. She began to coalesce into form, a body against his, contented puffs of warm breath against his face.

The following night they lay in a bed that mirrored his, existing in his mind.

More nights, flashing along at the rhythm of this pandemic, and the mirror world of the bed he made for them expanded. Her name was Anita. They'd met at a bar one evening, lonely drinkers. She'd been looking at him and he took the chance, they talked and he gave her his number. A few days later they got slices and beer at Boiler Room and he walked her back to her front door. Movie nights. Shows, museums. Sitting on her couch, reading sections from their favorite books out loud. She was living in a studio not too far away, and they both preferred hanging out there instead of in his frigid underbelly of an apartment. Her parents liked him—they'd been near to divorce like his own—and she was the middle child, he decided, all her other siblings were married with kids but like him she didn't want any of her own. When cases spiked they had movie marathons at her place instead of going out and like him, she fought back the feelings of abandonment from friends who were too busy or tired from it all to hang out much. But the sadness he'd seen in her melted, just a bit more, each time they were together and with it that presence in her grew, rising. He loved it. He loved her.

One night Ian lay down, thinking about the update Joel had just given him on his chemo treatments: they weren't working. As he slid into the world that he was building in his mind, he lay in bed with Anita and told her about it. She held him without judging him for needing to be held, and without saying that it would be okay, because she knew that you didn't promise things like that.

By the time he fell asleep in the physical world, the world within his mind had grown to encompass Joel a month from now: the cancer was going into steady, and optimistic, remission.

The next night his parents invited both him and Nadine to lunch on a Saturday. Despite worrying about another family fight, he brought Anita. And Nadine brought her partner. They sat out at an expensive riverfront restaurant, the kind of place you only went to for special occasions—which was already a good sign, it showed how much his parents wanted them back together. The three couples started off uncertain, but his parents were teasing each other and laughing again, holding hands, and they called Nadine by her real name, and they liked her partner—Ian liked him, too—and of course, everyone loved Anita.

Ian began looking forward to the night, to falling asleep next to her. He lay down in his bed sober, because it took longer to fall asleep that way and so it was longer he could spend with her, with them all, sliding into a world where they'd moved into a one-bed on the Boulevard that had central heating. The cold fell away, along with the mounting cases and Joel's worsening diagnosis and his parent's looming divorce—along with the whispers, the claws grinding bone, old monsters that had been robbed of his life. They lived in the basement shadows, components of a unifying darkness. They, it, had nearly had him, nearly driven him to it. And now felt cheated, wronged.

But he could avoid it, outrun it. He wanted to live again, but in this place with Anita, where everyone was happy.

In the fold of some night, just on the cusp of sleep, he chose this reality, and left the old one behind.

"I made you up."

"No. You made your own reality, your own world."

"This is pathetic." Ian fell back against the empty storefront wall. The living shadows were gone.

No, they hid inside of him. Gnawing. Waiting.

"I was so fucking hopeless that I had to make up a partner?" he hissed. "And a better life? I just... made this shit up so that I could control it all."

"You did it to survive," Anita said. "Otherwise you would've taken too many oxys on purpose, and slipped off into the dark with those monsters."

"I should've, for everything I've amounted to."

Ian.

They sat at the bar, just the two of them. Everybody else lay dead, their bodies slashed open, limbs strung across upended tables, blood on the walls and the bar mirror. Bits of shadow smoked upward from the wounds. Metallic tang of blood, mixed with the reek of spilled beer.

Yet Ian didn't feel sick or dissociated—he knew what that felt like, and this wasn't it. More like staring at a set-piece in a haunted house, just a lot of fake blood and dummies.

"The shadows?" he asked.

Sadness deepened Anita's face. "You created me for the same reason that you imagined Joel's recovery and everyone in your family happier with each other—because you need love, or the hope for it, like a weapon against reality. But—"

"But I'm not just that," he whispered. "My... hate, my rage at it all... made this, too. These monsters."

"You wanted to find good, but you also wanted to turn your hurt back outward."

So part of this reality contained monsters born from the slaughtering darkness. That were unstoppable, and tore apart imaginary victims who existed just to die.

And the shadow that had birthed them? Ian.

"Then why are they trying to kill me?"

"Because their master is the part of you that wants to die," Anita said. "It nearly had you, but then you made me, and the rest of this world, and you were happy again. So, it feels cheated."

Music played from the digital jukebox, but he didn't bother listening to the song. He was sure it was something he loved... and that Anita loved too, of course.

He said, "You're not real."

"But aren't I? You've pushed away the horrors of the reality you were forced into, and made your own. If anything, it's impressive."

Ian drank from a glass of Schlitz that hadn't been there a moment ago. It tasted so real... and the barstool under his ass felt real. So did the smell of blood.

He put his hand flat out on the bar, considered slamming his glass onto it. Would it hurt? Would his blood pool out over the glossy wood with that of his imaginary victims?

Something in him told him to try, to do it until the glass shattered. Then to pick up one of the shards and draw it across his throat.

He drank, instead.

Then said, "But you don't have any choice in this. I'm deciding that you love me. And that when we get to the Trevi Foundation I'll propose and you'll... say *yes.*" He frowned. "So if I decide that we no longer love each other, you'll be free."

Anita's eyes watered—why was he making her cry? They dried up. She said, "Of course you can. But I don't want that."

"You mean *I* don't want that."

"Because you need love, Ian. I'm the part of you that loves yourself... you need that, love, just like everyone else... no matter who made you feel otherwise."

"But nobody meant to. My feeling rejected is my... sense of entitlement. Like I deserve them, or anything."

"But you do."

He didn't like that, the affirmation, so he struck out against it. "This is just masturbation. Just... using myself for emotional pleasure, for love, for violent thoughts..." He leaned onto the bar and put his face in his hands.

Anita put a hand on his shoulder. "Ian..."

"Go away."

"Ian, come back to me—"

"Go away!"

III

Silence.

Just the gentle lapping of water kissing sand. Miles of Lake Superior shoreline, flat gray touching sunny sky. They'd come here on a family vacation when he was a kid, so he imagined it as he remembered it, filling in the gaps.

He decided that Rufus, his and Anita's Rhodesian Ridgeback, was here, too, padding around on the shore, skipping in and out of the water, biting at the waves.

Ian could make anything, really. How it all felt so real, he didn't know or care. That this had happened at all was easy enough to accept; with the real world falling apart and his life losing its foundations, why not sink into these fantasies so deeply that they became real?

But what was going on outside? What would happen when he woke up?

Did he want to wake up?

Anita's determination to keep him here was just his own determination, the part of him that wanted to stay like this—that shoved him into this world to keep him from killing himself in the one outside. But he was still a physical body, a brain in a flesh-suit that it needed to be sustained.

That was how bad it had gotten, he remembered. The physical world had just been the routine of working for enough money to give him a place to sleep, and for the food he needed to keep this brain alive. He'd taken to napping whenever he could, to maximize his time in this world. And he'd developed the irksome but not overwhelming trials he and Joel dealt with in small business ownership, and the occasional fights he and Anita had, and how the pandemic wasn't over but nearly so. At least he'd made it interesting. Everything good all the time was boring.

The shadows—*his* shadows—weren't here yet. Maybe they didn't know where to look.

He decided that Rufus needed a friend, so a dachshund named Cujo ran down to the beach and started playing in the surf. Ian himself had a beer in hand, a beach-chair under his ass and a portable speaker blaring some Dead. If he wanted to, he could make himself more muscular, and rich, a jetsetter without a care in the world. Just good vibes and love.

But what had he made for himself, instead? A solid, good life. Not perfect, but good.

He'd go back to Anita and his family and Joel later. They would keep. Right now, he was enjoying the weather, the lake, his dogs, and an aloneness that he'd chosen, not one that was forced on him.

beep ... beep
"You know what that is?"

He'd brought Joel in, sitting next to him in his own chair with his own beer.

"Yeah," Ian said. "Must be whatever they have me hooked up to, in the hospital. Guess I'm in a coma."

"You don't have to worry about sustaining your body anymore, then," Joel said. "Smooth sailing from here." His body had filled back in and he had a healthy tan, a head of long sandy brown hair like he'd had in college.

"I wonder, though," Ian said, "is it selfish, drawing in like this, while the real you is out there, dying? Shouldn't I wake up so I can be there for you—for him?"

"No. The Joel you left behind is so far gone that he probably can't tell who is and isn't around him."

Ian considered this. "Really, you're just the part of me that wants to stay here. I wonder what part of me wants to leave?"

And he was alone again. Which made sense: these were all fixtures invested in staying here. None of them would take his side.

"Well, duh," Nadine said.

Guilt spiked through Ian—she was the one person who he could help, even if she didn't always want it, or understand how hard he fought their parents for her. The last time he'd been on the phone with them, trying to reconcile things, their dad had said, "I just don't get where we went wrong with Jason." But that time, instead of screaming, Ian just hung up. What was she doing out there, as he played out this control fantasy? With her partner, and her friends who were like the family she should've been born into? Or was she shooting up again, hiding the trackmarks? He felt like she blamed him for something, but he was too oblivious to figure out what.

She said, "We're friends again, here." She pointed to their parents, walking out on the beach with Rufus and Cujo, holding hands. "And so are they."

"I didn't know what to do for you."

"What could you do? Were you really wanted around? Not just by me, but by anyone?" She sighed. "Thing is, all you have to do is just keep us here, and happy." A worried look crossed her face. "You'll keep doing that, right? I mean I know you make some problems, to keep it fresh, but you're not going to make it bad?"

"No," Ian said. "I don't want you to suffer."

But if he felt like a failure to her before, how utterly horrible was it for him to abandon her now, so that he could play pretend in this world?

His head hurt again. Like it was trying to expand.

"That's because your mind can't hold both realities at once," his dad said.

Ian.

"Who is that I keep hearing?"

His mom said, "Probably some nurse or doctor. I doubt it's anybody you know—the great resignation, people don't really care now. Any visits you've had were probably just an obligation, and all it's done is hurt your family—the one out there—even more."

"Even if I'm in a coma?"

"Well, who cared when you broke your arm?"

But Ian didn't trust this attempt at deflection—his own attempt at deflecting himself. "They're in the room with me, waiting for me to wake up... they have to be. You're lying."

"No, we're trying to help you," his dad said. *"You* are trying to help *yourself.* Stay here, and watch the rest of your life unfold into what it should be. What's back there, Ian? A pandemic, poverty, an overheating planet? All of that comes crashing down on you and everyone you love, you see it with every unanswered call, every cancelled date, every night somebody sits on their couch alone with a bottle in one hand and too many pills in the other. Honestly? More people should be doing what you are."

Ian.

His head swelled—pulled back in.

"But what about Nadine?"

"She doesn't want your help," his mom said.

"My parents? The real ones?"

"Like they're not too busy separating? They didn't really love you, you were just a duty for them. They only stayed together and suffered for it because of you. They'd have been a lot happier divorcing years ago, if you hadn't been born."

"What about Joel?"

"If you wake up and go to him, it'll only be in time to watch him die."

Ian tried to control the swelling and contracting in his head—but that was the one thing he couldn't get a mental fist wrapped around.

"It can end, though," his dad said. "You just need to commit to this."

"Commit?"

"By getting on the plane with me."

He stood at the gate. The concourse empty, lightless save the boarding screen's glow: *Gate K22 ROME. Last call for boarding.*

Anita stood at the jet-bridge, a tunnel of light behind her. She wore her shorts and jacket, her hair pulled back in a ponytail that opened her face, the beauty of her smile pulling at him.

"Get on the plane," she said, "and we'll go away. We don't ever have to come back."

The grinding darkness stood at gate K13. The shadows—*his* shadows, *his* darkness, *him*—waited. On himself.

He asked, "What happens if I go?"

"Then we'll spend the rest of our lives in a better place."

"I mean in the real, the *other*, world?"

"Does it matter?"

"It does to me."

She said, "You'll stay in the coma. Forever."

From the darkness came a whisper, a razor-wire threading into his mind. It told him to wake up, so that it could finish what it had started, before he created this world.

"What will happen to you if I leave?" he asked. "You said we'll all die... is that true?"

"I don't know." Bitterness in her voice. "Would it change anything, for you?"

"But I control all of this, so maybe I could—"

"You still don't *get it!*" she shouted. "Yes, I'm you, but I'm the part of you that loves yourself, Ian. I'm what freaked out and went into survival mode when the other part, when *that*—" She stabbed a finger toward the darkness "—wanted to kill you. Why do you think it's been following you? And slaughtering everyone? Because it wants you dead—*you* want you dead—so you're removing every reason to stay alive." She grabbed his hands in hers, eyes and voice pleading. "Which one do you really think is going to win, out there in the other world—in that horrible, disgusting place? Me? Or *that?*"

"Anita—"

"That's why we'll all die. Because that darkness will take you and make you end it... all of it, all the parts of yourself."

Her eyes held his, he could stay lost in them, in her—in himself. Yet he could give her everything: the successful career, all the travel she wanted, full days and fuller nights and a happy family and the perfect partner. The perfect husband.

All he had to do was get on the plane. And leave everyone else out there to their suffering.

But just because Nadine couldn't understand how he fought for her didn't mean that he should stop. Just because his parents were going to divorce, didn't mean that he wasn't allowed to be there for both of them in the aftermath. And just because Joel was dying, didn't mean that Ian had to act like he was already dead.

Because they loved him. No matter what the darkness kept telling him, their presence was still with him. Even if strained. Maybe that was love, at its most endurant: to simply be there.

... up

He couldn't tell who was speaking out there, but somebody was. One of them. Worrying about him, loving him, the best that they could.

"I have to go back, Anita."

She lowered her head, whispered, "Because you want to die."

"No, because it's real."

His head swelled wider and harsher than it had before and a blistering agony dropped him to his knees as the darkness took Gate K14. Then K17. K20.

Anita knelt and pulled him into her arms.

Gate K22.

It flooded over Ian and his head exploded—shattering the airport, scattering it into shards that flew glittering away into an indistinct abyss. Within this gaping hell-mist the suggestions of people and moments and emotions as vivid and real as what he'd left behind incandesced in and out of being. They grabbed at him, screaming for coherence, for a mind to guide them—a mind that wasn't fractured like this one but instead fully committed to the charade of their being. In the lowest depths, shadows reached up as demons from his own Hell—clawing not for control, but to facilitate the end.

A cloud in the shape of Nadine swirled by, dropped off into a heroin doze, vomiting, she needed to be rolled over or she would choke—Joel a withered shell of himself in a hospital bed, eyes emptying—his parents screaming at each other, at him, at Nadine—and the lonely man hiding in bed in a basement in the hell of winter.

Their voices joined with Anita's and with Rufus barking—congealing into one.

"This is what you'll return to," they said. "Suffering and resignation."

Ian. Wake...

Something was becoming clear—a physicality hardening into form, into pressure on his back.

"That world doesn't need you," they said. "It doesn't want you."

... up.

The pressure on his back was on his legs, too, and his arms and shoulders.

"They don't love you."

One of the real voices was Nadine's. He thought he could see her, sitting... by his bed. Mom next to her, holding her hand. And Dad on the opposite side.

Wake up.

He woke up in a hospital bed, cold under the thin sheets and listening to the simple *beep ... beep* of the monitoring machine. His parents and sister sat around him, tired and quiet. The only ones missing were Joel and Hailey. They were in a room in a different wing of the hospital, Hailey crying and Joel an hour dead. But for Ian that knowledge and hell would come later.

On this evening, two years into the pandemic and a week after going into a coma, he pulled himself out of it. And accepted this reality.

IV

Her life was perfect now. Except for when she thought about him.

Which wasn't often, considering how quickly Anita's life turned around—she'd gotten her own place, bringing Rufus with her, and kept busy with work and family and friends. On one of the first sunny days of the year—sometime in June—she met a guy at a party and after a few dates they both just knew.

Two years later, they were strolling the Riverwalk on the Fourth, heading to a slip where a friend's boat was moored; a bunch of them were going out onto the lake to watch the fireworks. They were drunk on the feeling in the air, holding hands that wore matching rings.

Her husband stopped to help a family with a broken stroller—he was like that, capable and kind-hearted. Anita stepped over to the railing to get away from the foot-traffic, leaning out over the water and taking in the downtown skyline and the harbor lock and the flat of the lake beyond.

And there he was.

Picking his way through the crowd, hands in the pockets of his jeans. He wore an old black jacket, no shirt underneath. And no sunglasses—but not like he needed them, really. And he wouldn't sweat, unless he chose to.

Anita gripped the railing, forcing herself to breathe. She smiled, just a little, the best she could. "Ian."

He leaned up against the railing, taking her in, matching her smile.

"How are you?"

"Do you need to ask?"

"No." He leaned back against the railing, taking in the crowd, the afternoon. "It's just nice to ask. Feels more authentic."

"It *is* authentic, to me."

They watched her husband right the stroller, push it back and forth a bit to test it, then give the parents of the babbling toddler a thumbs up.

"Why him?" Anita asked.

Ian said, "Do *you* need to ask?"

No, she didn't. "Because he's who you want to be."

"He's who you deserve."

"You know, Ian, sometimes you still think I'm a separate person." She fiddled with her ring, said, "Why did you do all this? You could have just... forgotten about me."

"You were there when I needed you—and I know, you're *me,* I made you—but I think I'm starting to get it. About different realities, everything you tried to tell me before. I couldn't stay with you, but this—" He indicated the world around them, her husband, the friends waiting by the boat. "—is the best I could do."

"Well," Anita said, "you did a pretty good job."

"Thanks."

"How are you doing, out there?" she asked. "How long has it been?"

He kept a casual tone. "Only a few days. We'll see what happens."

She didn't push him on it, or ask why he'd cut off her knowledge of the outside world. Instead she asked, "Will I see you again?"

"Probably not. I shouldn't come back here, you know? Kinda defeats the whole point of everything that happened at the airport."

Anita wished it didn't still hurt, but it was a generalized sadness, not the renewed heartbreak she'd feared. He'd already had her get over him, and she could sense that she'd soon forget about him, other than as the ex who left her at O'Hare.

"I hope you have this," she said, "one day."

"Me, too. But I won't until I go back to the real world. Fully."

83

Her husband swivelled his head around, spotted her, raised his hand and, grinning, picked his way through the crowd. Anita opened her mouth and turned toward Ian, trying to figure out how to introduce her husband to her ex.

But Ian was gone.

Anita didn't bother trying to sight him in the crowd. She took a breath, held a small smile, then broadened it for her husband as he took her hand and they walked on.

JUST A LITTLE TASTE

Samantha Lee Curran

You know the saying 'sink your teeth into' something? Well, I take that literally. Not in an 'I eat people' sort of way. I mean it is, but... let me explain.

Since I was an infant, I could be found putting everything and anything in my mouth – from slater bugs to toy cars and electronic devices. Anything I could get my chubby hands on went into my mouth. My favourite thing, though, was my parents' fingers. Like how parents stick their fingers in your mouth to feed you or put your dummy in. I hear you say that's normal for a child; but not when that child doesn't grow out of it and starts *craving* it.

I remember being nine years old and attending a birthday party for a girl in my class called Jasmine. Eleven girls gathered at her house for a sleepover and a pool party the next day. I had never attended a sleepover before and the thought of being around that many people in close proximity for an extended period sent panic through my body. We played all the typical childhood games – hide and seek, dressing up, tea parties and playing with dolls; frivolous activities that almost bored me to death. Although I was delighted by the interaction and to be included in such a formative experience, I wasn't feeling any sense of joy or contentment.

But then, we started playing Twister.

Twister unfolded like a smorgasbord of new possibilities to explore and inspect. Each time the colour wheel spun and I moved closer to another player, I'd feel my body tremble and my vision go blurry from unadulterated hunger. It took all my will to keep from nibbling on someone. The game only lasted about 20 minutes before we all gave up – but it seems like hours when you're desperate to understand the squealing girls just inches from your teeth.

By the end of the game, I lost all restraint. It was the first time I bit off a whole chunk of someone, and it felt like my brain went into slow motion and projected my future all at once. It was a euphoric experience, and I finally understood myself and why I had been living in such disarray. The girls and parents all screamed bloody murder. My parents were called to take me home, and those girls never spoke to me again. But I didn't need friendship, or to be understood. I stepped onto a different path, leading me towards an elevated comprehension of life and the world that no one else has.

Now, it's not what you think. I don't murder people to eat, I don't even need a human snack a day. I'm *not* a cannibal, I'm not barbaric. That shit's not my thing. I'm particularly sensitive about the word cannibal because it's *not* who I am. I just need to explore the world – and people – by having a taste. That instinct you have from infancy to put things in your mouth to inspect them just never left my body. I mean, the decadent flavour of human is a bonus... I'm thankful it doesn't make me gag like beef does.

Food has never been a priority for me. I know I have to eat for my body to thrive and survive, but I'm not one of those people who enjoys going out and trying different cuisines. I live in Melbourne, and if you've heard of it, you'd know it's essentially the foodie capital of Australia. People flock to cafes and restaurants in droves after work and on weekends to relish in the experimental hot spots that pop up constantly. Because going out to eat is the main social activity here, I tend to miss out on a lot of normal human interaction; socialisation, conversation, connection. The people in my life know not to bother inviting me to eat out. Brunch? For fun? Fuck that.

Since my twenties are on their way out, I thought it was time to begin looking for a romantic partner. I'd been feeling all the societal pressure of finding someone to share my life with, and I'll begrudgingly admit that I had been lonely. I'd attempted to find a partner before, but trying to navigate my curiosity in the dating world is not something I'd recommend. Most people can figure out whether a person is right for them within the first few dates, but for me, I can't exactly go around taking bites of people straight away. By the time I can, I'm already in too deep.

I met this guy at one of the many courses that I attend at the UniMelb. I try to consume knowledge in any way that I can – that doesn't involve ingesting body parts – to occupy my brain and curb my craving for connection. I already have a BA in Psychology, which taught me the intricacies of the human mind and emotion, and gave me a little more understanding as to why I might be the way I am. But there is always more to learn.

During my Uni course, I learnt about Hyperphagia. Hyperphagia is a condition in which people are controlled by insatiable hunger, where they never feel satisfied with how much they eat. This incurable starvation made sense to me, and I had hope for a while that I could decipher what was happening inside me. Although I wasn't dissatisfied with what was in my stomach, but with what I felt in my bones.

The guy's name was Dan. He was bland, dull, drab - no substance to speak of, and this drove me insane. He may have thought attending community courses would make him more interesting (surprise, it didn't). It was difficult for me to wrap my brain around how someone could live in this world and not have one captivating thing to say. It was easy for me to catch his attention, I think he was drawn to my perception and extroversion; maybe believing some of it would bleed onto him and bring him to life.

When we started dating, the two of us saw each other once a week; going out to dinner, movies, picnics - the usual shit. He would drone on about his childhood; only child, his parents still together, no childhood trauma - his job; a telemarketer for a paper company - and his hobbies; video games and tending to his lawn. Despite how badly I wanted to smash him over the head with a brick and get it over with so I could get my fix, I didn't. I couldn't. I won't. Dead flesh doesn't work; not that I'd be able to tell the difference with him either way.

Eventually we became close enough that I was comfortable with having a taste. The first time I took a bite, we had finally slept together and the uncontrollable urge to sink my teeth in took over. It wasn't a huge piece, but it was enough to chew on. Although he winced and whined like a child, he thought it was an exhilarating kink of mine and he seemed to get a buzz from it. But I felt nothing with him. No ecstasy pulsing through my body; no instant flow of heightened awareness; Nothing. It was something I hadn't experienced before. It mystified me, and only added to my curiosity. I was eager to try more.

If you're wondering, yes I've tried myself to see what would happen. It's like eating a piece of off meat; I violently gagged, got food poisoning and it felt like I actually *lost* some brain cells rather than gained any sort of wisdom. And no it doesn't hurt – that much.

It's not like I would have whole limbs or sections of him at a time. I'd take a mouthful, and that's all I'd need every few weeks. As I said before, I'm not barbaric. And he didn't seem to mind that I used him for my examination of human life. It must have added a slice of excitement to his own. But no matter how much of him I'd eat, I wasn't feeling any sort of high.

It appeared as if his flesh wasn't as potent as others, which could be a result of his mundane existence. I became addicted to the dissatisfaction, and the quest to reach the heart of it. I needed answers but I was merely getting a sample-sized KitKat each time. As I became increasingly frustrated at the lack of insight from him, he began to offer up pieces of himself voluntarily, maybe out of fear of me doing something rash. Of course, I took full advantage of this; never before had someone willingly allowed me to devour so much of them so I could discover more about them, and in turn the world.

That is when I began to try pieces of his thighs, stomach, arse; anything that was fatty enough to get a decent chunk, and hopefully a sufficient amount of 'vision juice', as I call it. To get what I needed, the bites had to be deeper, more substantial. I would feel my teeth sliding through his skin down to the bone. It was like biting into an apple, blood dripping down my chin.

However, it did become a problem within our relationship. He kept asking why I constantly needed a 'fix', and I could never answer. I didn't know how to tell him that I don't feel like a complete person. I am meant to be an amalgamation of people I meet - a puzzle with my pieces scattered and the only way to find the right ones is to try to fit anything I find. I've spent so much time searching for pieces that I tend to neglect whatever one I have in front of me.

I'm not oblivious as to why he was getting upset with me. I had become increasingly distant and uninterested in our daily lives. We barely spoke or interacted the way we used to. We were no longer getting intimate, I didn't even feel like touching him unless it was to munch on him. I began to become independent again; going out and not inviting him, making plans without considering him. It even got to a point where I didn't think about him most days, I almost forgot he existed.

It's difficult to consider others in pursuit of enlightenment. I'm purely driven by a lust for connection; a lust for understanding. I find that living in my head is *far* more pleasant than living in reality. And the moment after that first bite – twenty years ago at poor Jasmine's party – the world inside my head exploded into a kaleidoscope of ecstasy. To leave that is excruciating. It's *unbearable.*

We became strangers in our relationship, and for the first time, I saw something when I looked into his eyes. I think it was pain, and I knew that I had caused it. I was feeling confined by having a single possibility of living life, and frustration was oozing out of me and poisoning us. Being absorbed in one person until death isn't sustainable. Your mind and body become stagnant, and you create a loop inside of yourself that is almost impossible to escape. Most importantly, if you continue to live that way, you could end up killing each other.

After a while, he began to fade away, and all that was left by the end of our relationship was the parts of him I didn't fancy; the parts I had no use for. I can't tell if I was a more complete version of myself in the wake of it all, or if it was merely a grand illusion. But when he was gone, my world opened up once again to more tantalizing possibilities for insight, and I was prepared to devour them all.

I'm inquisitive and curious; I'm a consumer. But I'm *not* a cannibal.

JUST ADD WATER

Bill Link

Chapter 1

Jordan gripped the handle of the fire ax tightly with both hands, his heart pounding in his chest as his eyes, wide with fright, darted about the room, trying to find where *it* had scurried off to. The stark light of the battery powered lamp on the table threw his shadow from the peeling paint of the walls, to across the boarded up window, and up along the ceiling bulged and discolored with water damage, as did Arnold's body, still upright in his chair, his hands hanging lifelessly above the floor. Red, liquified flesh drenched his shirt from where his head used to be. The bottom half of his skull remained, with teeth jutting up from his lower jaw, along with the gaping hole of his throat down the center of his neck. The suitcase, which Arnold had brought with him, sat on the table top, it's lid open. The empty plastic water bottle laid on its side on the dirty, carpeted floor, nearby.

As he breathed in one ragged breath after another, all he could think about was how he didn't want to be there anymore. Fuck Jamison and his money, he needed to get out of there!

Faster almost than his eyes could follow, the tentacles scrambled the bulbous head across the floor from a darkened corner, making his heart leap into his mouth.

"*GEE-YAAH!*" He swung the ax through the air with a scream, slamming the sharpened head into the floor where the thing had been only a split second before. Despite the physical shock that had run up his shoulders and back from his arms, he frantically tried to pull the ax free from the floor boards, when he saw the creature squeeze itself bonelessly into a rat hole, half its size, at the bottom of the far wall.

"No! No! No! No!" he wailed as it disappeared. What was he going to do now???

Inside the wall, he heard the sounds of tiny rat feet scurrying about, followed by high pitched, squeals and screeches.

"I've got you now... whatever you are," he seethed, rushing up to the wall. Measuring the spiked side of the ax with the commotion behind the wall near the floor, he reared the fire ax back, then threw his whole weight into the swing as if he was on the golf course, punching a hole through wood and plaster with a *thunk*. The wall surrounding the hole was dented inward and crumbled with the blow. Yanking the ax free, he held the metal head before his eyes. The spiked side was covered with blood and blackish brown rat fur.

"Goddamn it!" He dropped down to the floor on his knees, and leaned his head down to peer into the hole he had made, his palms and fingers wrapped around the ax handle sweaty. Maybe he could just set the house on fire, his mind reeled for a solution. That way he wouldn't have to explain how

Arnold... His trail of thought stopped short when he saw the pinkish pupil set in a white-gray eye stare back at him from the other side of the hole.

"Shit!" he cursed, as tentacles squirmed out from the hole in the wall.

Chapter 2

It had begun weeks before, when Jamison had called his office. He had been in the examination room, fingering pressure points along the spine of one of his patients, Daryl Feldman, who was face down on the table, shirtless. "Now, doesn't that feel better, Mr. Feldman?"

"Actually, it sort of hurts worse," the older man complained, his head turned on its side on the cushioned table, trying to see Jordan over his shoulder as his brow furrowed with discomfort.

The phone rang from the receptionist desk. "Dr. Roger Jordan, Valley Chiropractic Therapy. This is Jessica speaking," the twenty two year old at the desk answered. "He's with a patient at the moment, but I can take... Well, I'll ask if he can speak to you. Let me put you on hold."

Jordan turned his head, distracted, his fingers now just fumbling around the man's backbone. After a brief knock, the door opened to the tall, strawberry blonde in the form hugging dress. The minute he had seen Jessica's sultry blue eyes and pouting lips, along with her long legs in the short skirt she wore when she came in be interviewed six months ago, he had hired her on the spot. Who cared if she hadn't done receptionist work before? How hard could it be to answer phones, he had figured. He had been fucking her on the sly since then, keeping her in tow with a minimum wage salary with promises he was going to leave his wife for her. How else was a short, middle aged man with a comb over like him going to get prime pussy like that on the side?

"Dr. Jordan? There's a Vince Jamison on the phone for you. He says it's urgent."

"Vince Jamison?" His eyes widened with surprise. "Patch him into my office." Taking off his rubber gloves and tossing them into the trash as Jessica turned away and closed the door, he said, "Well, we're done for the day, Mr. Feldman. Schedule another appointment with Jessica up front."

Struggling to sit back up, and grimacing with his outraged nerves between his compressed vertebrae, the old man shook his head in confusion. "But my back's still hurting." His face, reddening with pain, contrasted with his doughy, white torso and upper arms.

"We'll get to that two weeks from now," Jordan said, dismissively, as he hurried from the examination room.

"Hello, Vince?" he answered the phone in his private office, after closing the door. "What can I do for you?"

"That depends if you still got that contact at the EWU archaeology department," came the gravelly voice over the phone.

"I think so." He nodded.

"I have a buyer who's interested in purchasing certain fossils recently discovered on an archaeological dig in the Columbia Basin. This buyer is willing to pay good money for at least one such fossil."

"Well, how much are we talking about, here?" He leaned back in his chair to lift his feet up on the desk.

"Your cut would be six mil."

"Excuse me?" He swept his feet off the top of his desk, and sat up straight. "Did you say six million dollars?" He shook his head, certain he must have misheard.

"Six million. And I don't mean Pesos."

"Fucking Christ! Why is he willing to pay so much for... What? Dinosaur bones. Indian... I mean, Native American artifacts?" He ran his fingers through the strands of hair he grew long to brush over his balding pate.

"Shit if I know. But I don't get paid to ask questions, just to get certain items to my clients upon request. Now, take down some information, and we'll go from there."

Jordan had known Keith Arnold back in Idaho State University, twelve years before. Back then, they had stayed at the same dorm, he studying pharmaceuticals, and Arnold, an overweight kid with black rimmed glasses, had been an Archaeology major. Arnold had approached him one day, asking him if he had access to speed, suggesting they might be able to make good money selling to college students cramming all day after partying all night. And, yes, he had been able to get hold of Ritalin and Adderall in minute enough amounts that he thought wouldn't be missed. At the time, it had been mildly surprising for Jordan, as Arnold hardly seemed the type. But it took all kinds, he supposed. Other extra-legal opportunities opened up for the two. Soon, the two nerds were popular all over campus, making quick cash. He should have known it wouldn't last.

When he got busted, after his theft was discovered, he had been told he was lucky he was only getting expelled, with his scholarship rescinded, and not going to jail. After that, no legitimate college would touch him, and he enrolled in Chiropractic school, but never lost his contacts from Idaho State. For Arnold's part, he had been grateful Jordan hadn't ratted him out, promising he'd return the favor. That favor got called in when Jordan had treated a patient five years later, a muscular ex con named Vince Jamison for shoulder trouble after a bench press accident. They had learned much about one another through chit chat during sessions, when Jamison had asked if he knew anyone who could procure sundry, not-so-legal items for customers who valued discretion, telling him he could make good money as a middle man. Jordan could never say no to easy money.

Mostly, Jamison's clients dealt in drugs and contraband, though there were also a surprising number of collectors of antiquities willing to pay to to add artifacts to their private collections that otherwise would have been off limits. Most sought after were rare Native American grave goods that were otherwise illegal to purchase. That had been when he called his old friend and partner, Keith Arnold, who held a position at Eastern Washington University's Archaeology Department. Not only did Arnold feel a need to repay a debt to Jordan, but he wasn't one to kick cash out of bed, either. Soon, they had a racket up and running.

Jordan kicked back in the recliner in the man cave one he got home, and called Arnold. May was fussing around in the kitchen, making dinner upstairs. He listened to the phone ring, before a familiar voice answered. "Hello?"

"This is Roger Jordan. Long time, no see, Keith."

"You only call when you've got some deal in the works."

"I'm sure that's not true. But yeah, I've got a mutually beneficial proposal for you."

Arnold sighed. "Last time I floated some Clovis artifacts to you, I nearly got my ass in a sling. But let's hear what you've got."

"I have a contact who tells me he has buyers for fossils discovered at a dig at a spot near the Columbia, called Wolf's Head."

"That wasn't supposed to have hit the news, yet," Arnold's voice dropped to a hiss. "How did your... friend even learn about this?"

"Beats me. He just said he has a buyer who wants one of whatever's been discovered."

"I'm sorry, Rog, but from what I've been told, the secrecy around this dig is insane! I don't think I can even get near..."

"Your cut would be three million."

"Where and when do you want it?"

Chapter 3

Jordan answered the door to Arnold shortly after he heard the knock. Outside, Arnold's BMW was parked alongside his Mustang in the gravel driveway. The streets light illuminated the empty street, and the windows of surrounding houses glowed since night had fallen. "You're late." He put the lid back on his bottle of water he had been sipping from. After weeks of wating, Jordan finally had gotten a call from his old partner from their college days, saying how he had finally acquired the *item* in question.

"I figured I had the address wrong, so I drove past this place three times before I stopped," Arnold explained, huffing with effort as he lugged the oversized suitcase inside. The underarms of the heavyset man's button up shirt were stained with sweat. "When I saw the boarded up windows and the spray painted graffiti outside, I thought this house must be abandoned." Jordan closed the door behind him.

The abandoned house had been where Jordan had grown up, in fact, and which he had inherited after his folks had passed away. He had continued paying taxes on the property, but had cut water and electricity years ago. His wife thought he kept it for sentimental value, when in fact he used it for his extracurricular business ventures to avoid her prying eyes. Occasionally, he'd find vagrants or meth heads camping out inside, despite the *No Trespassing* signs posted around the property. In such cases, either displaying the fire ax he brought along, or a gun, got them leaving in a hurry. When the neighbors bitched the place was ruining their property values, and threatened him with a lien, he hired a starving artist type who ran a landscaping gig out of his pickup to mow the lawn and pull the weeds from time to time.

"Heavy?" Jordan closed the door, and led the way to a heavy legged kitchen table, where a battery powered lamp shined brightly from in the otherwise empty room. Their shadows moved across the water stained walls and ceiling as they approached.

"It's fossilized." Arnold looked at him, furrowing his brow with irritation. "It's a rock. Of course it's heavy!" Looking at the table, he said, "Over there? Here, give me a hand."

Setting the water bottle on the floor, then taking the bottom half of the suitcase to position it horizontally between them, Jordan helped him move it above the table, his own face red and straining as he felt its weight. *Shit, much more of this, and I'll need a good chiropractor!* he thought, almost with a laugh.

"Careful... careful, we don't want to shatter it," Arnold's voice was strained as they set the case down gently.

Breathing deeply, Jordan asked, "So, what makes this thing so Goddamn valuable?"

"Your business partner... didn't fill you in?" the heavy man panted, hard.

"He said he didn't even know." Jordan turned away for a moment to retrieve the water bottle from where he had set it on the floor's threadbare carpet.

"Mind if I sit down?" The heavyset man struggled to regain his breath, looking like he was ready to drop. Pulling out one of the two chairs scooted under the table, he plopped down. Wiping his brow, he held up a hand and waited for his breathing to return to normal before he spoke, again. "What we have here, inside this case, is going to change the biology books. It's fossilized evidence of complex life dating back to nearly a billion years ago, and that's not nearly the half of it." He patted the top of the case.

"Well, okay." Jordan shook his head. "What does any of that supposed to mean?"

"There is no previous evidence of anything alive that early. Least of all complex life."

"Let's just pretend I don't find that interesting at all."

"You're a man of science, aren't you?" Arnold held out his hands with a bewildered shrug.

"I'm a fucking chiropractor."

"Well, you haven't heard the main reason why this has been kept under wraps, yet."

"Which is?"

Arnold lowered his head and shut his eyes for a moment. "I can hardly believe the reports I've heard. They said, while cleaning off the fossils... When water was introduced... The fossils seemed to revive. Seemed to show signs of life."

Jordan's mouth fell open, and for a moment he was speechless. "You mean whatever you've got in the suitcase... comes to life with water... Just like those brine shrimp they used to sell in adds in the back of comic books, with the pink fork heads?"

"I suppose that's about as good an analogy as any."

"Just how many..."

"Fifty or more were discovered. The team at the dig believe there are probably more. And then there's where they were discovered, which is just almost nonsensical."

"You've got my attention. Where were they discovered?"

"Well, they were found inside the igneous rock. You know, the lava rock you'll find all over the inland Pacific Northwest."

"You'd think the things would've been incinerated by the lava." Jordan nodded slowly, beginning to understand the strange momentousness of the discovery.

"They said there was what looked like some sort of purposeful symbol carved onto the rock. You know... something that looked man made, as impossible as that is."

"What was it?"

"I'm told it looked like a leafless branch." He shrugged. "It got broken in the excavation."

"Open the suitcase." Jordan made a gesture with his hands, his interest peaked. "I gotta see this."

"You're sure your partner and his client won't mind?" Arnold's hands hovered over the clasps holding the suitcase shut.

"What they don't know won't hurt them."

100

Popping the clasps, Arnold pushed the lid open. Jordan walked behind him to see into the case.

"It looks like... an octopus had a baby with a jellyfish," Jordan leaned his face over Arnold's shoulder.

Inside the case was a crudely cut slab of rusty colored rock, on which was the distortedly flattened shape of a bulbous head, surrounded by a mass of tentacles branching from its bottom half.

Jordan unscrewed his bottle of water. "I can't resist," he said, smirking as he reached over the suitcase and poured out the water bottle on the fossil.

"What the fuck do you think you're doing?" Arnold grabbed at his arm to pull the empty bottle away with a wide eyed look of alarm. "Asshole! Is this the way you treat the shit I bring you?"

"Chill the fuck out! It's rock! What do you seriously think is going to happen just with a little water?"

"That," Arnold said with subdued awe, as he pointed at how the water seemingly was absorbed by the fossil inside the suitcase. Slowly, the hardened exterior cracked and fell away as a translucent, jelly like flesh began to rise like an inflating balloon. He slipped off his glasses, as if unable to believe his own sight.

"Holy fuck ... I can hardly believe it!" Jordan whispered. Arnold could only nod, his eyes and mouth wide with astonishment. Jordan had to wonder if Jamison's client fully grasped what he was purchasing.

"I can see organs forming under its skin," Arnold whispered, as a heart began beating inside the octopoid head, along with the growth of intestines and other innards before their very eyes. "I can even see a brain... and it's human sized! At least!"

As the tentacles began moving slowly about the stone slab in the case' interior, stalks, one after another, began emerging from the head, opening up to milky gray eyes in which pinkish pupils expanded. Those eye stalks rose upward past the case' rim, seeming to regard the two men observing them from above, as the boneless head slowly regained its spherical symmetry. It began making a gurgling sound, like a voice bubbling beneath the water.

Arnold turned his face up to Jordan, who had in the meantime walked to the side of the table for a different view of the creature. "This is the find of the century! Of the millennium!" he spoke rapidly, his jowls giggling with excitement. "Think of it! A sophisticated organism on earth, long before..." He stopped in mid-sentence when he saw Jordan's eyes and mouth stretch wide with fright, his finger rising to point at the open case.

Jordan hardly had enough time to yell, "Look out!" when Arnold turned back, only to see the creature springing out of the case, its slender, whiplike tentacles spread wide to wrap around his skull. He screamed as his head became a shadow, swallowed inside the creature's semi-transparent body, his fingers digging into its gelatinous flesh. Jordan reached out a hand, but hesitated, afraid to touch the thing, when he saw the shape of Arnold's head turn into a red cloud inside the creature, the liquified flesh draining into the recesses of its digestive track, seconds later.

"Oh God! Oh God!" Jordan sobbed, throwing his hands over his face to stare between his fingers, as he stumbled backwards. Arnold kicked about frantically, almost upending the light blazing from the tabletop. The thing pumped up and down, and shook as if in a sexual frenzy, as red, melted flesh oozed from its orifice-like mouth over his shoulders, drenching his upper arms and torso.

The ax! He had to kill the thing, save his friend if he could! Jordan almost fell as he desperately twisted around and ran for the fire ax he had left leaning against the far wall. Grabbing the handle, he spun around, wide eyed. And it was gone. Arnold's headless body sat upright behind the table, the suitcase open in front of him.

Where did it go??? his mind screamed, as he searched about the room for the creature. Dark shadows filled the corners outside the circle of bright light. His heart pounding behind his ribcage, he thought, *It couldn't just disappear... could it?*

Chapter 4

Jamison pushed open the door, and walked inside, the handle of the briefcase filled with money gripped in his hand. "Goddamn it, Jordan, I've been outside for the last twenty minutes, knocking on..." His cowboy booted feet faltered to a stop as he took in the blood drenched, headless body of the fat man seated at the table in front of an extra sized suitcase. Across the room was another blood splattered body sprawled out on the floor, which he thought must be Jordan, from the spindly limbs and loose fitting tee shirt.

"Holy fuck!" he breathed, his free hand sliding down from his shaved head down the front of his moustached face, and his eyes and mouth agape. He was a hard man who had seen plenty of bad things in his day, some of which he was personally responsible for. But this was something even he was unprepared for, as he walked gingerly past the corpse at the table to what he thought was Jordan. "What the hell happened here?" he asked no one in particular, as he stopped short of the body that laid flat on its back on the floor.

The eye sockets, nasal opening, and oral cavity were filled with blood thick with soft tissue that had spilled out over the face and hair onto the floor. His clothing was plastered in red to his body. A telltale trail of smeared blood, thick with tissue, was spread across the carpet from one end ot the room from the other. The fire ax Jordan used to frighten druggies and bums out of the house lay forgotten at the far wall.

Choking back on vomit when he felt his stomach lurch, Jamison reached for his semi-automatic tucked behind his waistband, under his leather jacket.

Jordan's head and shoulder's twitched, making Jamison step back with a gasp. *He can't seriously be alive!* Jamison thought, gathering his courage to lean over to look at the eyeless, noseless face. "Jordan...?" he asked hesitantly, bending his knees to squat down. God, it smelled awful! "Listen... I'll call someone to help. I've got doctor's who'll come and..."

Jordan's whole body began shaking, and his neck bulged outward as something moved from inside his chest. Blood exploded from the corpse' mouth with a flowering of tentacles into Jamison's face. He hardly had a chance to get a shot off, that reverberated in the empty house, when the creature enveloped his skull.

NEW YOU NANCY DREW

Chloé Sehr

I wanted it to be perfect. Really wanted to set the scene. I started a faux fire in the little glass box thingy in front of the defunct real fireplace. Those little plastic logs always gave the room a convincing glow.

After the package arrived, I was abuzz all day, cleaning and tidying the living room and dying my hair the perfect shade of red. The plain brown box was sitting on the coffee table until I was ready. I imagined a scene just like the one in *Moonstruck*. She gets home to her Italian-y house with all her shopping bags. No one else is home, so she has a fire-lit, get-ready date with herself before going to the opera. I wasn't going anywhere, but I wanted that cozy feeling, so I lit a cinnamon-scented candle and put it on a macramé doily I had put out specially, next to my bowl of cheese curls.

I changed into my best pink plaid PJs, poured myself a glass of pink wine from the box in the fridge and took a sip to calm my nerves. Then I put a Doris Day record on and settled on the sofa, listening to her wonder, *what will I be?*

I was ready.

I used a nail file to slice open the packing tape on the discreetly plain brown box. Pushing the packing peanuts away, I finally caught a glimpse of an adorable logo, a silhouette of a woman's head with a tiny nose and bobbed hair. A second sticker below that on the tissue paper read, *Nancy Drew 9*. Nine...nine...the ninth formula? Like Heinz 57? The rating, like, nine stars out of ten? The stickers contained no answers.

It all started a month ago, when I was in the vestibule of The Dramatic Dance and Drama Academy, after my acrobatic ballet/CrossFit class, *ABC for actors*. All that suspension from the ceiling really informs my acting. Anyway, I was getting in one last therapeutic neck roll in when I saw a notice on the bulletin board:

Actress needed to play Nancy Drew
Opportunity of a lifetime
Some pay

The bottom of the notice was cut into little strips with the same phone number written on each one. I guess they wanted me to tear one off, but I couldn't just leave all those other ones there where anyone could see and take one. I looked around. No one was watching, so I ripped the notice off the board and stuffed it in my bag.

My whole body was vibrating. Nancy Drew. My favorite character in all of literature. The one part I was born to play. This would make it all worth it. The starving, the acting classes, clowning, jazz, modern and tap classes, Pilates, Alexander Technique, therapy, restaurant jobs, all had led to this moment. After all these years of countless auditions and never getting a part, ever, no matter what I sacrificed to get it, I was finally getting my chance. I could just feel it.

I rushed home and dialed the number. The very nice lady at the other end of the phone call told me what to do. She said that this opportunity was so amazing that it required a small investment to weed out the lookie-loos and interlopers. I understood perfectly. She also mentioned that there would be some cosmetic alterations that would need to happen as well, but they would send me a kit to help with all that. Then she gave me an address and told me to send the money in cash and to include shipping and handling. She said to wait for a package in the mail that would contain the kit with everything I needed to become the Nancy Drew they needed for the project. When I asked what the project was, she said it was top secret and that she could tell just by the sound of my voice that I would be perfect. I thanked her and she assured me several times it was no trouble. No trouble at all.

It isn't exactly traditional to go about auditions this way, or to give a down payment first, but I thought, how is this any different from paying for all those classes? But it was quite expensive and she was very insistent that they only took cash. I smashed my piggy bank and sold the opal and diamond pendant I had inherited from my grandmother. It was hard, because it was the only thing she or anyone else had ever left me, but, like the sign promised, this was the opportunity of a lifetime. I gave my envelope of cash (including shipping and handling!) a little kiss for good luck and sent it on its way. I waited, and it took a good two weeks, if you can imagine, and I was so frustrated, but of course it was all worth it now that I was so close to becoming the new Nancy Drew! I would look just like her, I supposed. Would my new look give me sleuthing powers? The perfect sweater set? A gang of loyal friends and a handsome lawyer father? A father might be nice, but it all sounded pretty good to me.

And now, it was finally time. Sliding my fingernail carefully under the stickers on the tissue paper, I popped it open and saw a pair of pink dishwashing gloves (fancy!), a glass pot with the label, *New You Goo*, a tongue depressor from a doctor's office, a single green gumdrop in a small cellophane sleeve and a thick, rubber-like full-face mask that looked exactly, to the tiniest detail, like every drawing of Nancy Drew in every Nancy Drew mystery. I almost dropped it, it looked so real. Something in my stomach tingled. This was really happening.

Under all my new treasures was a handwritten card with instructions:
1) Eat spice drop
2) Secure hair away from face
3) Put on gloves
4) Apply goo to face with application stick
5) Attach mask to face
6) Leave on overnight
7) Do not call for help

Seemed pretty straightforward. I fluffed up the sofa cushions and ate my gumdrop, which had a spearmint taste at first, like a spice drop, but then something of an earthy flavor with a bitter aftertaste. Then I pulled back my hair with my lucky scrunchie and slid on a hair band to push back the baby hairs.

Goo time. The lid took a few knocks on the coffee table to get open, but then it came right off, emitting a pungent chemical smell that reminded me of the beauty parlor my mother had gone to on Thursdays when I was a little girl. We went there every week, without fail, until my mother had to go away. The woman that owned it had a beehive hairdo that looked like cotton candy. She kept nonpareils in a covered glass candy dish and always let me have as many as I wanted when my mother wasn't looking. To this day, it's hard to find anything as satisfying as the crunch of a nonpareil.

I carefully applied the very green goo to my face, looking into the hand mirror I had bought at the local secondhand shop. I felt like an heiress sitting at her vanity when I used that mirror. It was very pretty and nearly perfect, except for what appeared to be a cigarette burn on the back, just above the shepherd boy's head.

The combination of my dark green hair band and brown eyes, face shape and the very green of the goo made me resemble a large, animated avocado in my shepherd mirror, like I was a character on some kids' TV show. Avocado lady. Avocado detective. Avocado Lady Detective. Lady Dick, Avocado-Style. Solving fruit crimes. Because an avocado is a fruit, apparently. Did you know that?

Once the goo was on, it began to tingle ferociously, but if you know anything about beauty, that means it's working. The tingle grew very warm, then started to burn. I decided to be brave. Would Nancy Drew get scared that her face was burning off and go wash it off and ruin everything? No. She would bear the pain and see things through, no matter how tough or dangerous or painful it was. I took a deep breath, a sip of my wine, and picked up the special transformation mask that would make my Nancy Drew dreams come true.

The mask had eye holes and a mouth hole, so I could still drink my wine through the attached straw in my special wine sippy-cup, but it had no nose holes. I looked at it and wondered how it would stay on, as it had no straps. I hovered it about a half inch from my face and it...stuck. It stuck and stayed in place so quickly, it was like a vacuum sucked it toward my face. It was so firmly attached that I wondered how I would get it off when all was said and done.

The breath in and out of my nose was creating a tropical environment inside the mask. It was also intensifying the chemical smell. It occurred to me that they had missed an opportunity to make the cream avocado scented. Although to be fair, I'm not sure avocados have a scent. I tried to organize my breathing so that I only used my mouth, but I kept forgetting because the strangest sensation was traveling through my body and muscles and blood and arteries and I felt very calm. My face still burned, but I seemed to be observing it rather than actually feeling it now. Something was telling me to drift off, just sleep a little. That, plus the smell was getting so strong that I couldn't keep my eyes open. I—

-jerked up from my pillow. Everything was hazy. I was on fire. The room was on fire. I jumped up, then sat back down again. If I remembered anything from Mrs. Sarkey's second grade class, it's to not run when you're on fire. It will only feed the flames. I clutched my chest to calm my breathing and realized I was not on fire. I touched the sofa next to me, which was also not on fire. The only fire was my face. I lightly, lightly touched the mask. I felt the pain clear to the back of my spine, down to my feet and back.

What to do about a fire that has no flame to put out? Was this what hell is like? Always burning, no relief, ever? And who could I possibly call in a situation like this? The Fire Department wouldn't be much help if there wasn't any actual fire and in fact, they get quite angry being called to someone's house where there is no fire, believe me. Very angry. Also, I wasn't supposed to call for help, remember?

How long had I been out? The record player gulped and crackled at the end of side A. At least six songs. I stood again, determined to make it to the bathroom, but I couldn't really see. I mean, I could see shapes, light and dark, but everything was so blurry and my face was just so hot.

Then, there was a noise. Behind me? A rustling, then footsteps? A quick, sharp pain in my arm. I was falling asleep again. I heard a baritone voice as I drifted off:

"Goddammit. I told them the spice drops had to be stronger. But no one listens to me."

I always wanted to meet the *one* in acting class and be a power couple, like Lucy and Desi, but it never worked out that way. All the boys in my classes were arrogant and stupid and cared too much about their hair and how much they could bench press. Every day, unfunny boys who said they were comedians and untalented actors dying to be the next DeNiro were sucking up all the air in the room, getting on stage and acting like toddlers, with everyone saying how funny and great they were. Those were the guys that always got agents and showcases and always got cast in the hot indie movies. They barely looked at you when you had sex with them and then, the next day in class, treated you like an open sore. Then you see them years later in some picture, arm-in-arm with some idiotic Jessica Rabbit knockoff who does nothing but take and post pictures of different ways to eat avocado for the benefit of other idiots.

And the girls. None of the girls liked other girls. They were mean and none of them would admit to eating food. They all seemed to subsist on a variety of purple or green juice concoctions and fluffy-looking coffee they drank through a straw.

I guess acting is just a lonely life. That's what Bette Davis called her autobiography. *The Lonely Life*. I guess she'd know better than anyone. Is that what happened to Greta Garbo? She said she wanted to be alone, but maybe she just was alone, and lonely, and wanted everyone to think it was her idea. I get it. It's like, every day I have to create some story for why things didn't work out the way I wanted them to, and it's exhausting.

I woke up again to voices. There were two other voices talking to the first baritone voice. I somehow smelled cigarette smoke. I couldn't see anything. There was something covering the eye holes of my mask.

"Pink wine!" said a husky, judgmental voice.

"Who cares? She has the most snacks of any of them. Have you seen the variety of cheese curls? She really loves cheese curls." Perky-sounding. A familiar voice, I think?

Then, a crunching sound. Were there robbers in my house, eating my cheese curls, smoking cigarettes and drinking my pink wine? What kind of robber breaks into your house just to eat your cheese curls and drink your pink wine?

"Bess, stop it. We have work to do. Ned, stop standing around and help us." The Husky-Voiced lady again.

"Fine." Baritone.

I heard the sizzling of a cigarette extinguished in liquid. Were they putting out cigarettes in my wine, on top of drinking the rest of it, plus eating my cheese curls? How rude!

"She's almost cooked, but I can still see some of the edges. We need more time for integration," said Husky Voice.

"It's getting late," said Cheese Curl Thief.

"Yeah. No time. I mean, if the spice drops were stronger—" Baritone.

"Don't start, Ned." Husky Voice.

"It's like, I make suggestions, I say again and again how it is when I arrive on site, but it's like—" Baritone.

"No one cares?" Curl Thief. "I know. No one listens."

"Whatever you two are talking about, shut up and help me." Husky Voice.

There were hands under my arms, something I knew but didn't feel. I didn't really feel anything except anger about my wine and cheese curls. The fingers were skinny and poky. They would have bothered me if I could have felt them, but really, I was just aware of the idea that they would leave little poky bruises on my arms.

I was lifted to my feet. My knees buckled, but before I could fall down on the sofa again, two strong hands took me by the waist and held me up.

"I told you, after the shot, they can't stand up. That's why the spice drops have to be stronger. They knock 'em out at first, but later they can start moving around. We just need them to last longer. I keep telling them, but—"

"No one ever listens?"

"Yes!"

"That's because you're boring, Ned. That's why no one ever listens to you. You think small, that's why you'll always be a minor player in all of this. If this integration works out, which it WILL, we'll have the squad we need and I can lead us to the next level."

"Well, technically, you would be George, so the new Nancy would be the leader," Curl Thief.

"Shut up and help me, Bess."

They seemed to be arguing about some sort of military action, or at least spy operation. But why would spies be in my apartment, eviscerating my pantry and holding me up like a human corset? I think human, anyway. What if they were aliens? All of this would make a lot more sense if they were aliens. The real question is, do aliens eat cheese curls?

"The next thing we need to do is make sure these edges are smooth, so they integrate. I can't take all this waiting, then vetting, then we find one, then the integration goes to hell and we have to start all over. And after all that some of them aren't even "good enough" for Wax Division. And I hate driving all the way to the landfill every time we have a body we can't use. I'm sick of it!" said George, a.k.a. Husky Voice.

"That's what I'm saying. That's why I'm saying we need the spice drops to be—"

"Stronger, stronger. Yes, I know. You're like a dog with a bone, Ned. Just shut up and help me with her. Bess, what are you doing? Why are doctors always eating junk? Put down the cheese curls and help us."

Yes, Bess, put down the cheese curls. She'd been eating them for so long that at this point I wondered how depleted my supplies were. Had she eaten the traditional and the baked? What about the gruyere and seasonal port wine blend? Who was this cheese curl fiend? Excuse me, Dr. Cheese Curl Fiend. Also, I was very sure at this point that George was drinking all my pink wine. Perhaps the only one with any decorum was Ned, my human corset. As I had that thought, that corset was moving me out of the room.

I had tried so hard for so long to be myself, to let my inner light shine through, to be in the exactly right place at exactly the right time to be discovered, á la Lana Turner at the Rexall. It just never seemed to happen. I tried so many ways to be the best version of myself, to look the way they wanted. I needed to be skinnier, but I love cheese curls. So I ate cheese curls and salad for every meal. Whiskey made weekends disappear, so I switched to wine. Red made me sleepy, white made me hyper, so I switched to pink, my personal Goldilocks of wine. I could figure out anything, except how to get a part, any part, in any play, film, TV show, anything.

I read an article in Broke Actor Magazine about the life of that movie star from the 50s, Dorothy Dandridge. She once said, "have you ever caught sight of yourself by accident and you see yourself from the outside? That's who you really are."

Maybe she was right. What difference does it make what your innermost thoughts are or how good your intentions? Nobody cares. They take one look, make a decision about who you are and then punish you for not knowing what that is. Did it matter that she was talented? No. Even though she got famous because of her singing voice, they used a white lady opera singer in *Carmen Jones*. *Carmen Jones*! An all-Black film version of the opera *Carmen*! It didn't even matter that Dorothy was gorgeous. Every single person she knew thought she was either not Black enough or not white enough, a plaything or a punching bag.

There had been so many times I felt like I had made it, finally. There was the time at the commercial audition for Ocean Walk feminine products, when I asked the casting lady how to pronounce "douche" and she gave me a look, an odd look, curious, head cocked to one side, and I was sure she was envisioning me in the role that very moment. Nothing. Then there was the indie film about the gangsters and the mob and the big heist, when I read for a part that was a lady who goes around barefoot with a samurai sword. The director/writer/producer was so taken with me that he asked me to have a drink with him afterwards to talk about the part. He was a guy who liked to talk with his hands. He liked to do a lot of things with his hands. They were everywhere, which I thought would get me somewhere, but it didn't. Nothing did. Time after time, rejection, no matter what I was willing to do.

That's how I knew, the moment I saw that notice on the bulletin board, that my destiny was not to be a million sad, rejected versions of myself, but to become the ultimate version of the one role I was born to play—Nancy Drew. I would become her, body and soul, and I would get that part and finally be a success—finally go from *pick me, pick me* to *they picked me!* How could I lose? There's no way I could go to all the trouble of changing my looks, my whole life, and not get this part. I just knew it. Nancy Drew had protected me my whole life. Whenever I felt alone, as a kid, I could live in her stories for a while, hide under a blanket fort with some Lik-a-Mix and The Mystery of Whatever. As an adult, whenever I was blue after a bad audition, I would cuddle up with a Nancy Drew mystery, some pink wine and cheese curls.

But life is more than books. I'd never know if I would fulfill my destiny from my threadbare sofa. Whenever I couldn't afford tuition, my old acting teacher used to say, "jump and the net will appear." Well, this was me, jumping.

The mystery remained—why were these people here? Surely, if they had been sent by the production company, it would have been on the note with the instructions. Something like:

Please be advised that during the procedure, employees of our company will enter your house, poke you, hold you up like a corset, eat all your cheese curls and violate your pink wine.

Then all of this would be easier to understand.

Maybe this was part of the audition. They send people over to see if you're really committed. Well, look no further. I would let them put me through their little tests. I would prove I could go all the way. Let them prod me and push me around and set my face on fire with their goo. I would not be deterred. I would not be deterred. But I would need to sleep again, just a little...

"Ned, catch her! She's nodding!" I knew it was Bess talking, but there was something else...I knew that voice. Wait! Was it—

I woke up again and Bess was talking again, or still. "You know if she doesn't fully integrate, we'll be stuck in Wax again, doing maintenance on another dead-end body. Whatever happened to our dream of making it to Aerial and Tableaux

Division? They have bars there. And snacks. People dress up. It happens at night, so we could sleep in. No more nasty tourists with their sticky fingers and screaming kids."

"Bess, don't fall apart now. We're so close. All we have to do is control her and let the goo do its job. We can make it to Aerial and Tableaux. Maybe even...Spy and Sex Division. The top. Freedom. Our own missions. And most of all, no more of these ridiculous late-night chase-the-actress slumber parties." George, speaking in riddles, as usual.

"Bess, don't listen to her. They keep saying we'll get into A&T, just one more recruit, then one more, and one more, but it never happens. And everyone knows S&S is impossible. We've done everything the leader has said to do. We got them a Brenda Starr, all the Hardy boys, plus a Betty and a Veronica—" I hated to agree with George, but Ned was pretty whiny.

"Maybe Betty and Veronica don't count. We brought them in separately and Veronica has been nothing but trouble, trouble, trouble."

Trouble. Trouble. Why did that sound familiar? No trouble! No trouble at all! That's how I knew that voice. Bess was the lady on the phone! The one that sent me the package! What was she doing in my apartment? And what kind of doctor answers her own phone?

"Of course Veronica counts! The Leader knows how committed we are. Look at us. We've proven ourselves. We've brought more recruits than we even needed to. All we need to do to move to the next level is show them we have a perfect Nancy to complete our crew. All of us together will ascend to A&T. They can't deny us again. Besides, our recruits have already brought in a Dick Tracy and a Catwoman and are building their own crews. Do you want them to ascend before us? Do you?"

I felt cold, I think. I was in a different room now. And I was reclining. I felt around on either side of my legs and felt a plastic/nylon woven fabric wrapped around metal poles. A beach chair. I reached out to my right and felt a cool, hard surface. Tile. I was in my bathroom. In my beach chair. What was going on? Here's what I knew so far:

1) My face was still trapped in the mask.

2) I was sunbathing in my bathtub.

3) There were three strangers in my house: bossy George, whiny Ned and Bess, a.k.a. Dr. Cheese Curl Thief, a.k.a. the lady from the phone.

4) They worked somewhere with several acronyms and had a boss who wouldn't promote them or let them have snacks at work.

"Nancy. Nancy."

Was there someone else here?

"Nancy." she touched my arm. "I'm talking to you. I'm going to take off your blindfold."

She took off my blindfold and at first everything was so bright I couldn't really see anything but a dark figure surrounded by a circle of light. She came into focus slowly. Her hair was dark and parted down the middle. She took her index and middle fingers, smoothed a strand out of her eyes and held them to the side of her head to block out the light. Then I saw her bright blue eyes. They took me in and softened around the corners.

"I know you're scared, but you don't have to be. We're here to show you how you can never be afraid again."

Never be afraid again. The idea billowed through my mind. I thought about every scary movie I'd ever seen. I don't watch them very often, but even when you think you're just watching a dumb mystery show these days, it always gets so scary, especially the ones based on a true story. Nothing scarier than that.

In all these stories, there's a man who stalks. Mostly women are stalked, but occasionally it's a guy who just has the misfortune of unwittingly angering a sociopath by distracting the woman the sociopath would like to stalk. These sociopaths go anywhere they want, anytime. A dark alley where everyone gets murdered, not afraid. Dark house with spooky noises? Abandoned warehouse? Nothing. There are often scenes where this stalker waits in the shadows and watches his target. Maybe she's sitting on a back porch, trying to convince someone on the phone that she's not crazy, someone really is after her, as the stalker watches her through the slats of the porch railing, because he's after her. It must really be something to never look over your shoulder, because you're the thing everyone looks over their shoulder for. Freedom.

Is that what it takes to move through the world unafraid of the boogeyman? I had a friend in middle school who told me once that the secret to not having nightmares after you watch horror movies is to root for the killer. Is that enough to not be afraid, or do you have to become the boogeyman? Could George make me the boogeyman? Do I want to be the boogeyman?

"You look confused. Can I explain?" I closed and opened my eyes in a sort of nod. "You're Nancy now, or you want to be. Isn't that true?" It was George. Her voice was different now. Softer. "You can decide, right now, how much you want to be a part of this. You can come along with us and decide to be a part of the crew. Strategize, plan missions that lift up our leader and our cause. You'll be protected."

It sounded like a lot of work. I was disappointed. She must have seen it in my eyes.

"Oh. No, please don't worry. If that's too much for you, there's another way. We can make it so you don't have to make any decisions, have any stress, get all the pageantry of Aerial and Tableaux and then the prestige of Sex and Spy and never be worried about the little things."

I had no idea what she meant, but I needed to hear more.

Her voice got even softer. "What do you want? What do you really want? No one is looking. No one is listening. No one will know what you choose, or even better, that you had a choice at all. What do you want? We can just make it quiet for you, if that's what you want."

I had spent this whole evening thinking I hated her. But now, suddenly, she was the only one I wanted to talk to. I wanted to trust her. I wanted to answer her question. I opened my mouth and a little squeak came out. I cleared my throat as much as I could and got out the best answer I could with my uncooperative tongue and mouth.

"M-make it quiet for me. C-can't make decisions any-more. Just. Wanna. Be Nancy. Nothing else. So tired."

"I know. Don't worry. We'll take care of everything. Bess here can take you to the next level. Bess?"

Bess was a blond blur in the doorway and I'm pretty sure she was eating straight out of a bag of bleu cheese and lardon cheese curls–a very expensive late-night impulse buy from an import company favored by the French acrobats at The Dramatic Dance and Drama Academy. Would I have any cheese curls left after this was all over?

"Okay," said George. "I'm putting your blindfold back on now." I thought about protesting, but didn't have it in me, and then all was darkness again.

"Bess, it's time for The Procedure."

"I thought The Procedure was a last resort."

"You heard her. This is what she wants. We don't have to force her. That makes things so much easier. You know this. Now, it's up to you. You're what this team needs to ascend. You can get us to Aerial and Tableaux, where your whole world is the Moulin Rouge. Beautiful costumes. Playing to people in tuxedos, drinking champagne and martinis, and hardly anyone touches you. And if they do, at least you can tell yourself it's part of the show and it's not as bad. There are tips, gifts, things that make it easier."

"I know. I just don't–it's so-extreme."

"Do you know what they have in Aerial and Tableaux? Cheese puffs. And I don't mean bright orange toxic puffed air. I mean freshly baked, 1950s cocktail party, served in a tray by a housewife in a poodle skirt, little nuggets of joy. All yours. And all you have to do is your job. C'mon, Bess. you've trained for this."

"I didn't exactly train for *this*. I am a real doctor, you know."

"I know. And now you get to put all that training to good use. We can be a part of something. Aid our leader on his glorious quest."

"Well-"

"Bess, every time you say yes to our leader's plan, your life gets better. Every time you say yes, you get closer to what you want."

"I know. And I don't want to stand in anyone's way. That's not it. I want to ascend. It's just-it's the most primitive way. And everything should be sterilized-"

"--we're in the bathroom. We cleaned the bathtub. It's ready. We're ready. Are you?"

"I'm ready." She did not sound ready.

"Ned? Ned! Where are you? We're starting The Procedure!"

"I'm here."

"We need a shot. It's time."

"Yeah, okay."

George touched my shoulder and whispered in my ear. "Don't worry. Just a little prick, then you'll wake up and you'll have what you always wanted."

I felt the stick in my arm again.

I woke up. I looked around me. Nothing but light and color. A bright figure was walking toward me, surrounded by a halo of sparkling light. It got closer. It was a blond woman with perfectly coiffed hair, a dress with a poodle skirt and a spotless apron. She was smiling, carrying a tray of hors d'oeuvres, getting closer and closer to me. It was Doris Day. And she had a tray of perfectly baked cheese puffs. She offered them to me. I took one and ate it. I tasted nothing. I felt nothing. It was perfect.

DAN THE TRUMPET MAN

Mary Jo Rabe

Dan's hands shook slightly as he held the door open so that the rest of his brass quintet could march into the dark, little theater. The theater itself had seen better days, and the musty smell hinted at a lack of use.

Most of the wooden floor on the stage lacked varnish, and a number of the boards were cracked. The folding chairs behind the curtains looked rusty but perhaps capable of bearing the quintet's weight. Shabby appearance, but, as Dan knew from previous gigs, truly amazing acoustics.

He was cautiously optimistic about the venue and had every confidence in his quintet.

Mike, a tall and lanky thirty-five with short, curly, brown hair, carried his French horn case with two fingers as if it were a little bugle. Sherry, a petite yet compact twenty-five with short, blonde, straight hair, stumbled under the weight of her tuba. Steve, bald, average in height but with above-average muscle development for a fifty-year-old, squeezed his trombone case under one arm. Liz, a tall and skinny twenty-year-old with long, red, wavy hair, danced up the steps to the stage with her fluegelhorn in one hand.

A great bunch of musicians, talented, easy-going, and, most importantly, willing to accompany him to Mars.

Now it was up to Dan to see that they got the chance. He ran his hands through his thinning, short, light-brown hair and tried to collect his thoughts.

At forty, he was a good twenty-five kilos too heavy for his one meter eighty centimeters, wore rimless glasses, and loved music. He judged himself to be a better-than-average trumpet player and, according to his own estimation, a brilliant composer who, however, always needed new inspiration.

Lately, Mars sounded good for that. An aging multi-billionaire was still recruiting colonists for his thriving settlements on Mars and paying all the costs, but everyone knew that he was choosy about the people he selected. Dan needed to persuade the old gentleman to send this brass quintet to Mars along with all the instruments.

Thinking about the fact that this brief performance today might be his only chance to get to Mars increased his perspiration and heart rate, not good since he soon needed to perform the trumpet concert of his life. Dan shook his head and hoped his research on Mr. Baxter's musical tastes would turn out to be correct.

As his band arranged the instruments on the stage, Dan stumbled through the seats in the front rows, searching for the best spot for Ned Baxter to sit. The worn seats creaked, at least those that weren't broken, but Dan hoped he'd found the optimal location. The loud and clear sounds of his quintet warming up helped to decrease his anxiety.

In the middle of Dan's musings, Mr. Baxter, a wrinkled, little old man, so old Dan had no idea what his age could be — apparently unlimited funds could keep a body functioning as long as desired — dashed in, reminding Dan of a hyperactive, little garden gnome.

"Well, I'm here," he said in a high-pitched, squeaky voice as he chose his own seat in the front row and sat down. He stroked his meticulously trimmed, triangular, white beard.

"Don't get your hopes up," he said. "I may be paying for this Martian adventure, but I'm not throwing my money away. Why should I transport musicians and heavy instruments when it costs next to nothing to send digital music files if my colony decides it wants music?"

"That's why we invited you here," Dan said as he ran around the aisle to get to the front row. "You have probably heard recordings of music, maybe even of brass quintets. But if my research is correct, you have never been to a live concert. I'm betting that our live concert tonight will convince you that your people on Mars need musical instruments and live musicians."

Then he ran up on the stage, and the quintet began to play, loudly and confidently.

It turned out that his research had been spot on. Way back when, as a teenager Mr. Baxter had played the drum in his school's marching band and had retained a love of marches. After the quintet's impassioned rendition of the *Washington Post March*, followed by *Anchors Aweigh*, the members of Dan's quintet had their tickets for Mars.

"I might even visit the red planet myself to hear you again," Old Ned screeched

It didn't take all that long for Dan to find a promising venue for his brass quintet's performances on Mars, Eddie's Barsoom Bar and Grill, some ten stories below the Ares habitat administration area.

"What do you think?" Dan asked the others when he showed it to them.

"Hmm," Mike said. "Great location. This far underground means no neighbors can complain about the decibels. It's huge. I wonder how the Martian rock walls will influence the acoustics."

"Yeah," Sherry said. "We won't know that until we practice. It's nice that the stage area is more than big enough. The rest of you won't have to crowd around my tuba."

"I'm guessing that we'll be able to adjust to the acoustics," Dan said. "I'm probably prejudiced, but I really like the looks of the place."

"Yes," Liz said. "It reminds you of clubs on Earth, but it doesn't let you forget that you are on Mars."

"The lower gravity won't let me forget that," Steve said. "I keep stumbling into things."

Dan was relieved that the group found Eddie's place acceptable.

The tavern was kept comfortably cool, dark, and dust-free. Customers sat on low bar stools around sturdy, Martian-made, plastic tables that resembled tree stumps with flattened tops and a maximum of three stools per stump so that the guests always had plenty of room for food and drink and an unobstructed view of the stage area.

The whole Ares habitat from the surface dome down to the tenth underground story was of course pressurized and had its own air supply that was constantly recycled, cleaned, and humidified. Still Eddie's bar was the only location in the whole habitat without the pervading stench of hydrogen peroxide from the dust on the Martian surface.

Eddie, whom Dan almost never saw after their first negotiations, was ageless, as well as tall, gaunt, and probably suffering from a mild albinism, judging by his snow-white mane and reddish eyes.

More importantly, though, Eddie loved music and was always on the lookout for passionate musical entertainers. After their audition, he offered Dan's quintet an unlimited contract. "I'm sure my customers will love you," he said. "You're good, and you love what you do."

Eddie was right. After a little practice, Dan's quintet wowed the customers, most of whom longed for familiar Earthie tunes, though. Dan's group played pop and rock music, marches, spirituals, country music, everything that the people in Eddie's establishment requested.

Eddie paid them generously in Martian credits, and the enthusiastic customers soon started leaving excessive tips specifically for the quintet. It seemed that everyone in the Ares habitat and occasional visitors from other habitats desperately needed live music in their lives.

"What do any of you do with all the money we get?" Liz asked after a rehearsal.

"I haven't figured that out yet," Steve said. "Dan, you got us one good deal with all the living expenses automatically paid for by the settlement."

"Old Ned doesn't throw his money away, but he believes that you get what you pay for," Dan said. "Myself, I'd like to experience more of the planet. That was why I wanted to come here in the first place. Why don't we use some of our money to go on the expensive tourist tours? They have balloon rides and rocket jaunts. You can take guided tours of all the Valles. There is cave and crevice spelunking. You can even ski down the carbon dioxide drifts at the poles."

Sherry thought for a moment. "Actually," she said. "We should make videos of all these activities and set them to music. Dan, you wanted to compose new stuff here. It's time you started."

"All a matter of scheduling," Mike said. "So far we have rehearsed every morning, but I think we have enough routine now that we can keep our performances just as good without practicing every single day. Let's go explore the planet."

Dan had always been aware of how lucky he was with his quintet. The people were much more than just ambitious, talented musicians; they were completely on his wavelength.

They spent the next Martian year exploring everything the planet had to offer. After each trip, Dan retreated to his apartment and composed a new piece of music, the next one wilder than the one before. His works were like nothing he had ever thought of on Earth. The landforms and landscapes, the weather cycles and processes, all hauntingly alien, inspired him.

Unfortunately, the crowd at Eddie's Bar and Grill never liked Dan's music. They listened politely when the quintet played Dan's newest composition at the end of the show, but they only ever requested Earthie melodies.

However, Liz and Sherry set up recording equipment at Eddie's. They added the quintet's rendition of Dan's newest compositions and amplified sounds of the Martian winds to the videos they made from scenes when they traveled around the planet. These videos sold like crazy on Earth. People there said the videos made them feel like they were on Mars and they loved the "genuine" Martian music.

Sections from his *Phobos Fantasia* became theme music for films. His *Tharsis Rhapsody* won awards. Poets competed for the chance to write lyrics for his *Arean Concerto*.

In their spare time, Mike and Steve got involved in habitat politics. Mike noted that herding cats would be easier, but they made themselves useful, preventing regulations that would have interfered with Eddie's Bar.

After Dan and his group had been there a little over a Martian year, things changed slightly. One evening after the last performance, Eddie, who generally stayed in the shadows, came over and offered to buy Dan a drink. He motioned for Dan to sit at one of the front tables as the crowd left.

"How are we doing?" Dan asked, wondering if Eddie had complaints or if he wanted to adjust their working agreement.

Eddie brought two glasses of a sparkling red liquid that turned out to be a tart, chilled, juice concoction from the habitat's own orchard and sat down next to Dan.

"I'm pleased," Eddie said pleasantly though strangely noncommittally. "Ever since your quintet started playing here, this place has sold out most evenings."

"That makes us happy, too," Dan said. "Musicians need an audience."

"It is considerate of you to do requests," Eddie said. "Perhaps you have noticed that settlers on Mars, although one might expect them to be adventurous explorers, are fairly nostalgic and conservative when it comes to the music they want to hear. When they come into this bar, they are more into memories than listening to something new."

"I have to confess that I don't quite understand that, but musicians know that they have to keep the customers satisfied," Dan said. "We always start off with requests and tend to try out our new songs late at night when the crowd is somewhat inebriated and no longer pays such careful attention to what it is hearing. I still keep hoping that they will request the new stuff someday."

Dan was actually very disappointed that people on Mars didn't like his Mars-inspired compositions, but by this time he and his quintet were getting rich from their Earth sales. And he hoped that the next generation of Martians might like his stuff better.

"Good thinking," Eddie agreed. "You also don't want to try unfamiliar, new songs in the afternoon when the physicists show up. They listen even more than they talk, and they only want to listen to music they heard on Earth. They say it helps them clear their minds so that they can return to their physics musings and come up with new ideas."

"Glad to help," Dan said uncertainly.

"Unfortunately they don't drink much either," Eddie continued. "But they keep coming back."

Dan tried to look interested but he wished he could figure out where this conversation was going. Fortunately, Eddie finished his drink and focused his pink eyes on Dan.

"You're just a brass quintet," he began. "Don't get me wrong, you're great at what you do, but have you thought about including more musicians and instruments, and increasing your repertoire? I've had requests from people who would like to join your band."

Dan took a too large gulp of his juice drink and inhaled a few drops, causing him to cough uncontrollably for a few seconds.

Once he could breathe again, he said, "No, so far I've just thought about us playing here and my composing new stuff, but sure, I'm open to expanding our group."

"Perfect," Eddie said. "Trusting that you would agree, I already ordered additional instruments from Earth, and they will arrive in ten Martian months. A few months after that, Mr. Baxter will be sending us an Elvis impersonator."

"Great," Dan said. "How did you get Mr. Baxter agree to spending more of his money on additional musical instruments?"

"That was the Elvis impersonator," Eddie said. "It seems he is quite persuasive when it comes to getting what he wants. When would you be ready to audition additional musicians?"

"As soon as the new instruments have arrived," Dan said.

Dan and his band, now including a piano, saxophones, flutes, and clarinets, was practicing when Eddie came in with the Elvis impersonator. The man looked like videos Dan had seen of the 1970's Elvis, and his voice was a perfect match. Dan put down his trumpet and walked over, offering a handshake.

"Hi, I'm Dan the trumpet man," he said. "And how do I address you?"

The man smiled with the slight Elvis curl of the upper lip. "Awfully polite of you to ask, Dan," he said. "Thank you. I have had my name legally changed to Elvis the King. Please call me Elvis and feel free to refer to me as the king."

Dan nodded, and Elvis continued, "Then I suggest that we take care of business. I'd like to start performing here tonight, if it's all right with you. Which of my songs can you play?"

Fortunately forewarned, Dan and his band could play every single song the original Elvis had ever sung.

Eddie's Barsoom Bar and Grill became even more popular. Dan's band now played on occasional afternoons, opened for Elvis in the evening, continued to play during the Elvis show, and then closed with his Martian music after Elvis left the establishment. It was a perfect arrangement.

Elvis got Eddie to invest in a robot lighting technician that was programmed to spotlight Elvis perfectly, brighter on his face, darker on his torso. After consultation with Mike, Sherry, Steve, and Liz, Dan said that the robot should leave the band in the shadows. They agreed that the audience should focus on the music they heard and not the faces they might see.

When Elvis sang, the guests always sat spellbound. After each song, naturally, they yelled out requests, and they only wanted to hear familiar Elvis hits. Dan's band soon no longer needed to rehearse the Elvis show. Elvis just handed Dan a list of the songs for each night, all songs the original Earth Elvis had recorded and his fans had loved.

To Dan's genuine surprise, it wasn't boring playing the same music every night for Elvis, mainly due to Elvis's performance. The man threw himself completely into the role and reacted immediately and believably to the customers behind the tables. For them he was the reincarnated, genuine Elvis.

The Mars Elvis was quite a few Earth years older than Dan, but they became good friends. They both believed in taking care of business and keeping the customers satisfied, even though Dan still wished his late-night customers were more open to new songs.

Many Martian years went by. When the alien underground cities on Mars were discovered, Dan had even more new inspiration for his works. His *Pavonis Mons Opera* was an eight-hour tribute to the beings who had once settled the planet a billion years ago and left their works of art when they left.

Dan bought his own surface vehicle and started driving himself around. He had the feeling he still didn't know enough about his new home planet. The more he saw, the more he wanted to compose. Dunes, rocks, dust devils, and even the dust-filled, wispy atmosphere became new inspirations.

The emotions he felt driving along the Valles Marineris became the basis for his *Martian Sonatas*. The red, brown, and black rocks were as genuinely alien as the crevices, canyons, and mountains.

Once he was caught in a dust storm for hours and crashed into a surface habitat building. The maintenance people were not happy, but the swirls of dust in the air became the theme of his next symphony. Another time, a dust devil some hundreds of meters high chased him home, which resulted in the *Dust Devil March*.

Hiking over the North Pole and skiing over the frozen carbon dioxide at the South Pole resulted in a trilogy anthem, his *Snow on Mars* movements. The original quintet played everything Dan composed as passionately as if they had written it themselves.

Since he was doing so many new things, Dan didn't mind playing oldies in the Barsoom Bar and Grill. University fight songs and familiar marches continued to be especially popular. However, the king of popularity continued to be Elvis the King, who put on an impassioned show almost every night. Even Dan had a hard time remembering that he was only an Elvis imitator.

After a number of Martian years, though, Dan noticed that Elvis had to cancel performances more and more often and was spending weeks at a time in Doc Brach's clinic. Elvis seemed to be having problems with his vocal cords. One night his laryngitis was so bad that he couldn't get a single sound out.

A few days went by, and then Dan got a message from Elvis saying that the doc said he probably couldn't ever sing again.

Dan could imagine how this devastating this must be for Elvis. He took a robot habitat transport vehicle, a spiffed up dune buggy with a robot at the wheel that drove through the tunnels faster than any sane human being would attempt, to Elvis's apartment. After he pressed the exterior button to request entrance, Elvis opened the door and let him in.

"Sorry," Dan said as they went into the compact sleeping/living/eating area that stank of peroxide dust with a hint of a famous sweet alcoholic drink from the genuine Elvis's home territory. "Are you sure you won't be able to sing again? I mean, I thought the doc could fix almost any health issue with his little, internal nanobots."

Elvis sat down on the red fold-out couch and motioned for Dan to sit on one of the genuine, green Earthie beanbag chairs. "Everything has been repaired too often," Elvis said in an uncharacteristically quiet voice. "There is no substance left, just scar tissue. I can talk, and my speaking voice can get a little stronger, but singing just won't work anymore." Elvis seemed to be lost in thought.

Dan made all the suggestions that occurred to him, Elvis could try lip-synching. He could introduce holograms of his performances. Dan didn't want to believe that that this problem had to mean the end of Elvis on Mars. The audience loved him too much. Elvis listened politely but looked sad.

"I have to quit," he said quietly, trying not to strain his voice. "If I can't give the audience my best, I don't want to perform at all. You'll have to get back to rehearsing a whole new show without me. Thanks for stopping by."

Dan didn't have a good feeling about leaving, but it seemed that Elvis did want to be alone. He rode the terror-inducing robot vehicle back to Eddie's where Eddie was waiting for him.

"Too bad about Elvis," Eddie began as Dan entered the bar. "Ever since he got here, I told him that his body couldn't take doing a show every night. Imitating another voice puts enough of a strain on human vocal chords. Too much strain, and ..." he paused and rubbed his pink eyes discretely.

"However," Eddie continued. "Over and over again Elvis pointed out that his contract allowed him to sing as much or as little as he wanted. He had persuaded Ned Baxter that every planet needed its own Elvis, and that he was ours."

"Well," Dan asked. "Should we continue playing Elvis songs every night like we did whenever he was sick?"

"Yeah," Eddie said. "But you can gradually add more requests and ease into your own show sooner."

"What about hologram performances?" Dan asked.

"No way," Eddie said firmly. "My customers get genuine live entertainment. I have every confidence in your band."

Their Elvis tribute shows worked out well for a while; by now the audiences were used to Elvis not always being there. After the shocking news that Elvis had managed to eject out of a rocket and become a permanent — to the extent that anything on Mars was permanent — satellite, never leaving the planet, things changed. Dan and his band played nothing but Elvis songs for a memorial week.

After that, the interest in the band's Elvis music became more sporadic. Dan and his group still began every evening performance by asking for requests. At first most were for Elvis songs, but gradually people got back to requesting the other songs they felt nostalgic about.

Dan asked Sherry and Liz to accompany him when he drove his surface vehicle around the habitat. He wanted more visuals that were a perfect match for the songs he composed when he saw something new to him on the surface.

However, since both of them didn't feel safe when he drove — completely unreasonable on their part, he thought — he got the habitat mechanics to install video cameras inside and outside the vehicle that he could operate by himself when he was driving.

One dusty evening he had some trouble with the video equipment and then forgot again that the horizon on Mars tended to mislead an Earthie's sense of distance. The horizon was always closer than you thought. Thinking about his next composition, he drove over the edge of a crevice some several hundred meters deep.

Mike, Sherry, Steve, and Liz knew Dan would want his body to be cremated on Mars — with the dust set free on the top of Olympus Mons where some of it could sink to the Martian surface and the rest could take flight into space and out into the rest of the universe. Mike and Steve were able to get the habitat administration to agree to the arrangements.

Just as many people came to Dan's memorial services as had come to Elvis's. Unfortunately, Steve and Mike, despite their positions on the habitat council, couldn't prevent old Ned from dictating all the details of the service.

The service was to be broadcast to Earth, and Ned was still paying for most of the colony's expenses. After a request from Eddie and less than subtle pressure the incompetent Mayor Ben Berry, they had to submit to Mr. Baxter's orders, beginning with the selection of the farewell music.

Instead of any of Dan's many original compositions, Mr. Baxter insisted that the band play "Stars and Stripes Forever", arguing that Dan had died out among the stars.

Mike, Steve, Liz, and Sherry felt Dan's dust shuddering in the Martian wind and hoped he could forgive them, wherever he ended up.

CONTRIBUTORS

Arthur Davis is a management consultant who has been quoted in *The New York Times* and in Crain's *New York Business*, taught at The New School and interviewed on New York TV News Channel 1. Over a hundred thirty stories have been published in eighty journals, featured in a collection, nominated for a Pushcart Prize, received the 2018 Write Well Award for excellence in short fiction and, twice nominated, received Honorable Mention in *The Best American Mystery Stories 2017.*

Nick Young is a retired award-winning CBS News Correspondent. In addition to *Dark Horses,* his writing has appeared in more than two dozen publications including the *Pennsylvania Literary Journal, The Unconventional Courier, Bookends Review, the Nonconformist Magazine, Sandpiper, the San Antonio Review, Flyover Magazine, Pigeon Review, Fiction Junkies, Typeslash Review, The Best of CaféLit 11* and Vols. I and II of the *Writer Shed Stories* anthologies. He lives outside Chicago.

Victoria Male (she/her) has worked in creative development at The Montecito Picture Company and Graphic India. Her prose has appeared in *The Chamber Magazine.* A shrewd adaptor of biography, history, and mythology, Victoria seeks to celebrate the complexity and the breadth of the female gaze in her work.

Terry Sanville lives in San Luis Obispo, California with his artist-poet wife (his in-house editor) and two plump cats (his in-house critics). He writes full time, producing short stories, essays, and novels. His short stories have been accepted more than 500 times by journals, magazines, and anthologies including *The*

American Writers Review, The Bryant Literary Review, and *Shenandoah.* He was nominated three times for Pushcart Prizes and once for inclusion in *Best of the Net* anthology. Terry is a retired urban planner and an accomplished jazz and blues guitarist – who once played with a symphony orchestra backing up jazz legend George Shearing.

Wayne Kyle Spitzer is an American writer, illustrator, and filmmaker. He is the author of countless books, stories and other works, including a film (*Shadows in the Garden*), a screenplay (*Algernon Blackwood's The Willows*), and a memoir (*X-Ray Rider*). His work has appeared in *MetaStellar—Speculative fiction and beyond, subTerrain Magazine: Strong Words for a Polite Nation* and *Columbia: The Magazine of Northwest History,* among others. He holds a Master of Fine Arts degree from Eastern Washington University, a B.A. from Gonzaga University, and an A.A.S. from Spokane Falls Community College. His recent fiction includes *The Man/Woman War* cycle of stories as well as the *Dinosaur Apocalypse Saga.* He lives with his sweetheart Ngoc Trinh Ho in the Spokane Valley.

John Stadelman is a writer from North Carolina now based in Chicago. He holds an MFA in Creative Writing from Columbia College, and his horror fiction has appeared in Full Metal Horror, Schlock!, Lovecraftiana and elsewhere, and he is currently at work on a novel. Although he doesn't believe in ghosts, he's pretty sure he saw a Chupacabra one night on the North Side. Stalk him on Twitter at @edgy_ashtray.

Samantha Lee Curran is a poet, writer and founding editor of *trash to treasure lit.* Her latest poetry collection 'exposure to existence' was published in 2023 with Alien Buddha Press. Her work can be found in *Stereo Stories, Mamamia, Anearkillik, SourCherry Mag, DED Poetry, Soft Star Magazine, Spiritus Mundi Review,* and *Missive Mag,* among others. Samantha was chosen as a Vessels of Love poet for the inaugural City of Sydney poetry event and was an Artist in Residence at Chateau d'Orquevuax in 2023. Instagram: @s.l.curran Twitter: @slcurran

Bill Link is a lifelong resident of the Spokane/Spokane Valley area where most of his fiction takes place. He has published two novellas in the horror and weird fiction genre: *Skin Like Tanned Leather* and *At Night Outside The Window,* as well as three anthologies of his short fiction, *Creeping Shadows, You're Always With Me And Other Stories,* and *Six Times The Terror.* He lives with his wife (and best friend), their daughter, and their cat, Lovecraft.

Chloé Sehr is a writer, teacher and storyteller of all kinds. She contributed the forward and an essay to *The Cocktail Guide to the Galaxy* by Andy Heidel and was a recipient of a short story scholarship at the Stonybrook Writers' Conference in 2013. She previously co-hosted and co-produced the storytelling show, *WAX: Stories on Vinyl* and currently does the same for the show, *2short2suck*. Most of the time, Chloé is an ESOL teacher at Brooklyn Public Library, Brooklyn Community Services and CUNY Kingsborough. She lives with her fiancé and two cats, Gin and Tonic, in Brooklyn, NY.

Mary Jo Rabe grew up on a farm in eastern Iowa, got degrees from Michigan State University and the University of Wisconsin-Milwaukee. She worked in the library of the Archdiocese of Freiburg, Germany, for 41 years and retired to Titisee-Neustadt, Germany. She has published "Blue Sunset", inspired by *Spoon River Anthology* and *The Martian Chronicles,* electronically and has been published in *Dark Horses Magazine, Pulphouse, Fiction River, Penumbric Speculative Fiction, Alien Dimensions, Fabula Argentea, 4 Star Stories, Wyldblood Magazine,* and other magazines and anthologies.

Made in the USA
Columbia, SC
17 May 2023